Brooklyn UNLEASHED

A NOVEL

BROOKE DEAN

ISBN: 978-1-962870-16-0

Written by Brooke Dean

Published by Brooke D. Dean

www.brookeddean.com

Distributed by: IngramSpark

Dedication

To Jax, my greatest creation. My reason. Thank you for being my daily motivation to make something better for the both of us. The joy you bring me can't be measured in words. Thank you for giving me the most important, wonderful, magnificent, perfectly blessed title ever…*Mommy*. I love you.

CONTENTS

Chapter - One...1

Chapter - Two..11

Chapter - Three..21

Chapter - Four...31

Chapter - Five...41

Chapter - Six..49

Chapter - Seven..57

Chapter - Eight..67

Chapter - Nine...75

Chapter - Ten..83

Chapter - Eleven...91

Chapter - Twelve...99

Acknowledgments

This is my second novel, yet writing the acknowledgments always seems to be the hardest part! Probably because there are so many people to thank that I don't want to leave anyone out. However, God will always be first on the list of "thanks" as nothing is possible without Him. Ever present and always guiding me, I am grateful for the abundant blessings He has bestowed upon my life.

To my son Jax…the dedication said it all. My heartbeat.

To my family, thank you for your unconditional love and continued support. You all are the grounding force in my life and give me balance.

To my dear friends - sisters (and brothers) in love – thank you for the shoulder, the feedback, the pep talks and for allowing me to share my passion with you. You all really make me believe that I can do this thing!

Thank you to all the other authors in my life who have shown me love, respect and support. I am your biggest fan and I'm thankful for all the insight you all have given me throughout this journey.

To anyone who has bought, downloaded, read, shared, liked, loved, interviewed me, spread the word or wished me well with my first novel Brooklyn Unbound, your support has not gone unnoticed and I thank you from the bottom of my heart. It means more than you know.

CHAPTER

One

I've been thinking a lot lately about the Brooklyn I was versus the Brooklyn I want to be.

The version of myself I knew intimately before today was unsure and repressed, constantly riddled with guilt over the nature of her own needs. She couldn't relax. She couldn't accept joy and pleasure for the celestial gifts they were.

As I stand in that dim bar looking between my newfound crew and J, the beautiful man who holds my heart in the palm of his hands, I truly understand all the ways in which I'm not that Brooklyn anymore.

Not the same terrified woman who met J all those months ago on a BDSM dating app. Not the version of myself who was so afraid in the beginning. J taught me so much and opened up an entire world I never knew existed.

Now I realize that I love to give and receive pleasure, in more ways than I ever thought possible. I'm not ashamed about it. And my heart is still open to love in real, tangible ways to a person I deem worthy of it.

Most of all, Brooklyn 2.0 doesn't give a fuck about what anyone else thinks of her life or decisions, and she'll be damned if she can't have it all.

Why? Because damn it, I deserve it.

Which is why I slip my hand into J's and smile up at him, hoping he can see in my eyes how much I still want to be with him.

"Come with us?" I leave it as a question, an open invitation for J to either accept or reject. I leave him choices because that's what he's given me. I'm not willing to do any of this if there's any doubt that J is no longer looking for what I'm willing to offer. I have enough clarity now to understand that's not the kind of relationship dynamic I want.

I watch him glance over one of my shoulders at Darren and Adonis – and no, I have no idea if that's his real name but with the way he's built, I certainly don't care – the two funny guys I've fallen into spending a lot of time with who both also happen to fuck like they're being paid professional wages to do it. Adonis, the younger one, took it upon himself one night to help me explore the intensely pleasurable nuances of back-door entry. Darren, older with his graying temples but just as attractive, helped turn me into a deep throat pro. The three of us vibed together so well while I was here exploring the group on my own without J. We tended to consistently gravitate toward each other. None of them had ever done me dirty and I trusted them implicitly.

J looks over my other shoulder at Claudine, the curvaceous older woman I met several months ago with a French name and a Middle Eastern accent who still looks like an exotic model despite the deep crow's feet around her eyes.

The heavy bass of the house music pumping through the building's speakers makes the polished wood beneath our feet thump against our soles as the four of us stare at J expectantly – me with my heart stuck solidly in my throat because I honestly have no idea what he's going to say.

Then, like a miracle, he squeezes my hand and smiles. I can barely breathe while I wait for him to speak. "Sounds like a party," he says in that throaty grumble I love so much.

Hallelujah.

I want to jump up and cheer, but Claudine beats me to it with an excited squeal. I don't think anyone in my crew has been with J before; and judging from the way they look like they could eat him up, all three of them are looking forward to it.

Claudine practically skips over to J's side and grabs his free hand. Her gigantic breasts look like they're going to tumble right out of her top; you can see the darker outer edge of her areolas peeking over the low neckline. "Let's all go get a drink!"

Sounds like a fabulous idea to me.

As we stand at the bar and wait for one of the busy bartenders to mosey on down to our end to take our orders, I glance at J at my side. He's quiet, more so than what I consider normal, and it's making me a little nervous. What if he doesn't want this after all? What if he's only agreeing to do this for my sake and might resent me for it later? I don't want to feel like I'm coercing him into a situation he doesn't want to be in.

Currently, my boldness has abandoned me and I only nudge him with my elbow to ask what he wants to drink with a shy little smile, one that is completely at odds with my whorish attire.

He shrugs, glancing back and forth between the two gentlemen and lady in my group, and I see him trying to figure out how my young(ish) ass became a part of their little clique. Such is the magic of the BDSM scene, I suppose – bringing unlikely folks together as friends and fuck buddies. I stopped trying to understand it long ago. Considering J has been a part of the life much longer than I have, I'm surprised he seems to find the uniqueness of my group so intriguing. Intriguing is better than disgusting, I guess.

I smack some cash down on the counter for the bartender and get J the same drink I ordered – a neat cognac because I'm going to need all the chill I can possibly get tonight. J's presence alone is starting to spike my anxiety, and sex is hardly fun if you're trying to do it stressed out.

"To our Brooklyn," Darren says by way of a toast, holding his cocktail up high and practically shouting to be heard over the loud music, "the belle of our little ball tonight." He pauses to wink at Claudine. "You came in a close second, my dear."

Claudine laughs, breasts jiggling as she does. "It's a concession I can make," she says as she clinks her crystal glass against his.

The rest of us follow suit and I down my shot in one fiery swallow that makes warmth bloom in my chest. I instantly feel sticky under all this latex.

I've barely put my glass back down on the bar when Claudine sidles up to me with that saucy grin of hers, sliding a hand around my waist to cup one of my ass cheeks. "What –" I start to say, but she's kissing me deeply before I have a chance to react, and with the height she has on me, those jugs of hers are right under my chin and pressing on my throat.

All I can taste is cinnamon and some kind of fruity wine while my heart jackhammers in my chest. Now, Claudine is a woman who knows what she wants – a quality I admire in her – but Jesus Christ, I didn't expect her to pull something like this right in front of my man…

Her tongue has already invaded my mouth and retreated before I'm in a headspace to respond. And then… she half turns to hook a hand behind J's neck and gently pulls him down for a kiss, too.

Lord.

To my shock, J's eyes close and he kisses her back - his full, soft lips molding around hers like she taught him to do it just that way. The tingling triggered between my legs as I watch them makes me uncomfortable enough to squirm where I stand.

This is… okay. I had intended to ease into this a little more slowly, but clearly Claudine has other ideas. My eyes widen when her free hand moves forward and strokes the front of his trousers and he releases the tiniest moan I can tell he tries to bite back.

I'll be lying if I say I'm not beyond turned on and obscenely jealous at this point in time – I absolutely am – but I'm still worried about J's reaction to all this.

When I look up at him, however, he lifts his eyebrow before flicking his gaze in the direction we need to go to head downstairs. "Are we doing this or no? We're waiting on you."

I grin. Well, if he's truly on board…

Threading my clammy fingers through his, we follow Claudine and Darren – sometimes exclusive lovers, I've learned – and we all weave through the crowd writhing to the music playing throughout the mansion to the staircase that leads to the underground play space I now know like the back of my hand.

No one has on any mysterious masks tonight like the first time I attended one of these events with J. Honestly, I don't even know what the theme is or if there's one at all. Judging by the lack of participants wearing costumes of any kind, it seems like everyone here right now showed up to have a plain old sexy time without any frills.

I'm okay with that.

All the alcohol the five of us have consumed must have left us keyed up and eager to get started, because no one even pauses to check out the happenings in the occupied glass-walled rooms on either side of the wide, carpeted hallway. Normally, I like to take my time and browse the viewing rooms to see what kind of trouble I'd like to get into on any given night, but right now I'm so slick and horny, I can barely walk normally. My body is all about *participating*.

Even though there's a pretty good turnout tonight, there are a couple of empty rooms available. Claudine and Darren select the nearest one and J, Adonis, and I follow.

Each room downstairs has an entirely different set-up, with some featuring paint and décor with a jungle or cyberpunk theme. Others are plain with little more than a poster bed with a rubber sheet and a table full of every kind of manual sex toy you can imagine. The room my two friends selected appears to be one of the latter. I spot a bed, a small trunk against the wall opposite the window I presume has been prefilled with sexy accoutrement, and a random electric fucking machine in a corner that makes my mouth water just looking at it. I've only tried something like it once – with Adonis, actually – and I squirted like a Roman fountain for the first time in no time at all. In fact, I came *too* fast, but I haven't yet had a chance to see if I can hold out longer on a second go.

Shit. J catches me staring at it and I feel a pang of guilt that he wasn't the one to introduce me to it, just before I forcefully remind myself that *he* had been the one who flaked on my invitations time and time again. He could have been here with me to try all these new things and decided not to, so he certainly can't judge me for wholeheartedly embracing the full experience.

My three highly sexual companions are totally clueless to my internal conflict, having already set up shop on the bed while J and I stand there watching them and looking lost. Claudine croons as Adonis towers over her and fondles her breasts with both hands, all while Darren tilts her chin up and gently ravishes her mouth with his own.

My breath starts to come quicker and I'm sure anyone looking can witness my previously soft nipples turn to pebbles in my tight top.

I feel a literal gush of fluid soak my panties when Adonis and Darren start kissing Claudine at the same time in a sensual triad of wet, stroking tongues as their collective moans begin to grow louder.

God… that is so *hot.*

It never ceases to amaze me how capable my mind and body are of reacting to new arousal triggers. I used to think that sex was the good old in-and-out and that's all there was to it, but becoming part of this community has proven to me time and again that I was very, very wrong in that assumption. There are so many ways to stimulate and be stimulated and honestly, I don't think I'll ever learn them all. Plus, all that sampling is half the fun.

Evidently, J is at least as stirred by my friends' lusty performance as I am. He turns my face toward him, gathers me in his arms, and practically makes love to my mouth. He does it with an intensity I don't expect – which is saying a lot, because nearly all the time we've spent together has been intense in one way or another since the day we met. It feels… I don't know. He holds me like I'm delicate enough to break, and his lips move over and envelop mine with such fervent passion I can no longer breathe with the regularity required of someone actually trying to stay alive. Good thing he's holding on to me the way he is because I'm pretty sure I've lost the use of my legs by now. Despite the circumstances, J kisses me like we're the only people in the room – no, the only people on the planet. In the *universe.* It's the kind of kiss that makes you want to have a man's babies, and I feel so safe. Safe enough to let my guarded heart off its leash.

I wrap my arms tightly around his neck, falling into him, giving in completely, not caring about any potential consequences down the road. Here and now is all that matters.

As he so often does, J reads my mind and picks me up so I can also wrap my legs around his waist and growls into our kiss, making me whimper in response. Our noises mingle with the sounds coming from across the room, but I can't tear myself away from J long enough to see what those three are doing. Between the spiced decadence of J's cologne and the heady taste of liquor we're sharing between our tongues, my entire body is on fire. I want J more now than I think I ever have. I can barely stand it.

Even with both of my hands holding his face captive to my kisses, J manages to deftly reach under my tiny skirt and rip one side of my equally tiny G-string. The taut fabric snaps free of my thigh, making the whole thing slip uselessly to the side. Not that they were covering much, anyway.

Both of us are breathing hard when J puts me down and falls to his knees in one smooth motion, pushing at either of my calves until I finally catch his drift and shuffle my feet further apart.

The moment I make enough space, he dives between my glistening thighs face-first.

J works at me down there for a few seconds at most, but my knees are already trembling. His tongue goes from soft to firm and back again as he works his way in and around my folds, briefly circling and sucking at my rapidly swelling clit before retreating to start the whole maddening process all over.

I can't help it; my hips are already bucking over his mouth and chin. It's been so long and he feels so good…

J isn't ready to be done with me yet, so he *literally* flips me upside down when he stands back up and gives me easy access to his crotch to distract me. *When the hell did he learn to do this?*

With my mouth watering, I unwrap his package like the gift that it is, unzipping his fly and tucking my fingers under the elastic band of his underwear to push them down and out of my way.

His girthy thickness springs free, gravity helping it fall right down into my waiting hands and open mouth. He's savory and delicious on my tongue as I swirl it around the head in a way that makes him breathless, and all I can think is how much I've missed being with him like this.

I don't get to bob my head and slurp away for long because the trio on the bed finally remembers we're there and calls out for us to join them.

I'm convinced J has been hitting the gym overtime. With me still upside down with my legs around his neck, he walks us over to them like I barely weigh a feather. He gently lays me down on my back atop the mattress, leaving me slightly disoriented.

J is still standing over me, and through his spread thighs I can see Darren and Adonis making out. I slide down a little to get a better view, only for Claudine's naked and prowling form to fill my field of vision. Her dark curls are already wild, mussed by two sets of male hands.

She tosses me the most wicked grin before she plants her soft hands on each of my knees to press my thighs apart.

When she lowers her head and starts licking my pussy like I'm a melting snow cone, my hips buck hard on their own accord. She is so good at this. All the while, J's hands stroke up and down my trembling legs.

Holding on to either of J's upper thighs, I'm drifting away on a cloud of ecstasy.

I find myself slammed back to the erotic earth when J, now having shed his clothes completely, bends at the waist and joins Claudine in her task from the opposite direction.

Holy God in heaven…

It takes a moment for me to realize that the mewling cat sound I hear is coming from *my* throat.

With Claudine probing my wet opening with the tip of her tongue while J suckles at my clit… it's almost too much. My back arches and relaxes in tandem with their combined movements and I can feel the peak of pleasure tightening its fist around my spine.

I whine in protest when Claudine withdraws, but I pipe down when I realize she's only moving to the side to give J the space he requires. He's come around to her side of the bed and I watch him climb onto the mattress on his knees with stars in my eyes.

He yanks my hips toward him and impales me on his stiff cock with a grunt for himself and no warning for me. Wet as I am, he slides right in, but the force of it still hits me like a ton of bricks and makes my lungs emit a loud squeak when it steals my breath completely.

J is merciless, forcefully coaxing my body to accept every last one of his generous inches. I cry out when he pulls me back toward him with both hands, each time I try to keep him from bottoming out on my cervix. Eventually, he smacks a firm hand against my sternum and holds me down so all I can do is lie there and take it, my hands reaching for something – anything – I can grab onto to keep my sanity intact.

I have no idea what the hell I'm reaching for. There are no sheets on this bed and while Darren and Adonis are staring at J and me with wide eyes and stroking their cocks while they watch, they're both too far from the bed for me to touch.

Claudine easily solves my problem by angling her ass on the bed toward my face and grabbing my wrist before pushing my three middle fingers deep inside her softness.

Oh, God.

CHAPTER

Two

A loud curse fills my mouth at the feeling of Claudine's slick, soft heat, and I pump those fingers with no prompting needed, fucking her from behind with my hand while J destroys my womb in the most wonderful way possible.

Claudine yelps in time to my thrusts, which happen to be right in sync with J's wild strokes. I'm panting so hard my throat is bone dry already, but I can't keep quiet if I tried.

Darren and Adonis seize the opportunity created by my consistently wide-open mouth. J's wild fucking has pushed me so far across the mattress, my head now hangs conveniently off the other edge. Adonis is the first to reach me and rubs his wide head over my lips, still puffy from J's earlier kisses. I stick out my tongue and he chuckles, giving it a couple of healthy whacks with the bottom of his hefty dick before I eagerly take him down my throat as far as it will go.

From this angle, I can't see J at all, but I can feel his eyes on me, hot as a brand across my bare stomach. Does he like what he's seeing, this new side of me?

He must because J suddenly shifts right to hit that spot deep inside and wrenches a scream from the depths of my soul. Darren has maneuvered his manhood directly into my hands. It's already plenty wet and slick from his own saliva and precum, so all I have to do is squeeze and stroke his length and he's purring like a kitten.

For a good long moment, everything feels so good we all stay exactly where we are: Darren's hips flexing into my hand, Adonis' cock pumping my throat, Claudine riding my hand on the bed, J fucking me into absolute oblivion.

I'm the center of their sexual universe and I'm loving every second of it.

J has become the de facto conductor of our sensual orchestra and pulls out of me to make some changes. The two other men step back from me to stroke each other for a while. In the wake of their retreat, my heavy-lidded eyes pop open wide when J looks right at me and seizes Claudine by the waist, pushing her head down into the mattress. She roars like a lioness when he enters her from the back. But he never looks away from me.

The ferocity in J's eyes makes me bold. I sit up and begin making out with Claudine right in front of him, our tongues gently warring with each other for dominance. I groan into her mouth. The fact that my man and I are technically inside of her at the same time… it's hands-down the most erotic thing I've ever experienced.

Darren wants a piece of the action between us ladies. He climbs on the bed and straightens onto his knees, his cock jutting straight out like an accusatory finger. Claudine and I instinctively reach around to cup each of his ass cheeks and pull him closer so we can both lick him at the same time. I can taste myself and his own unique flavor as Claudine and I slide our parted lips wetly up and down his shaft.

J never stops pounding away at Claudine, her rounded ass rippling like a wave with each of his punishing thrusts. He doesn't stop looking at me either, and I can tell by the way his grunts start to deepen in tone that he likes what he sees.

He's accepting this. Not once has J tried to stop me or suppress any of my passion. Just knowing this opens up something inside me, something I have been keeping locked down and away from the light of day.

I don't know what it is or what to call it, but I even surprise myself when I gently push Darren away from myself and J away from a squealing Claudine so I can flip her over onto her back.

I remember how to speak for the first time since we began when I narrow hot eyes at J. "Don't stop fucking her," I say, and he thrusts back inside of her without breaking eye contact with me, which almost makes me come on the spot.

Swinging my leg over, I sit up on my knees and ride Claudine's face, who happily clutches at my backside. "Kiss me," J says, his rough voice riding up and down my spine and producing shivers I can't control. I vaguely hear Darren and Adonis getting nasty somewhere behind us, but I'm too dazed with need and J's attention to turn and look. I practically throw myself at him, and while his hips continue to piston his stiff flesh into Claudine's yielding body, his hands are free to rip the remaining bits of latex that comprise my outfit off mine.

I try to relay to him with tongue and lips and moans everything I'm feeling that I can't express with words. He kisses me back with the same sense of urgency and I think he understands what I'm trying to say. At least, I hope he does.

J curses loudly against my lips after I lower a hand to circle Claudine's clit and she comes with a holler almost instantly. Her pussy is clenching hard enough to milk J of all he's got, but he doesn't give in to the temptation.

He and I move back enough to allow a breathless Claudine to slide out of our way, right into the waiting arms of Darren, whose grin tells us all that he wants his turn with his woman. She's on him in an instant, swallowing him deep in her throat with no trouble at all, the intensity of the pleasure she's providing making the man hiss like an angry snake.

I feel like I'm drowning in a sea of carnality and I've never been so turned on. The ache deep inside my body is almost painful.

My hands tug at J's shoulders until he turns and sits on the bed, and I position us so I'm straddling him.

A contented sigh escapes me as I sink onto him, taking him as deep as he'll go, watching with fiendish delight when his eyes flutter and roll back into his head. J's hands find my hips in silent encouragement, and I ride him to the salacious soundtrack of Adonis' rhythmic grunts as he jerks off while watching us. Claudine's screeches while Darren fucks her with his entire fist.

J stares up at me like I am a goddess descended from above to grant his every wish and desire. I certainly feel like one right now, rolling my entire body over his in time to his deep thrusts. His eyes are as glassy with lust as they've been all night, but now, I see something else as well. It's like he's finally letting me see a tiny piece of the part of himself he'd always hidden from my view. A raw vulnerability that makes my heart ache and my hips move faster. I feel like I've been invited to break his being if I so desired.

Adonis doesn't afford time for the existential wanderings of my mind. He moves to stand behind me and the second his soft lips touch my neck; the vulnerable look J gives me fades away because he and I both know what Adonis wants.

I don't kiss him back. Not yet. I need to be sure that J and I are on the same page.

Unblinking, he bites his lip and nods once.

It's so subtle, no one else would understand, but I do.

I turn my head and capture Adonis' lips in a heated kiss, staring at J all the while. I don't stop riding him. Adonis doesn't ask me to, easily catching up to the pace I've set as he applies a generous squirt of lube to his tip and works his way through my back door.

There's so much intense pressure, I have to consciously force my body to relax as it tries to make room for Adonis' entry. He works himself in, inch by inch and the burning stretch I feel gradually becomes a pleasure so powerful, I can barely keep from screaming every time I lower myself down around J's pulsing cock.

The room is now a chorus of guttural moans and grunts. Adonis is still a few inches shy of being fully seated inside my asshole, but I'm so full to the brim, I can't move anymore. J stops with me, his hands wandering my stomach and breasts, leaving a trail of fire across my sweaty skin. I stay in one spot with my eyes clenched closed. Adonis reaches around and hits me with a wet, lazy kiss, groaning long and low once he's in as far as he'll go.

My entire body shakes. J pants beneath me, still as stone. He's inside me so deeply, I can't tell where my being starts and his ends. It feels like we're one person. Even in spite of the fact that Adonis has picked up the pace behind me and started a long, deep stroke in my ass that gives me clear visions of the monstrous orgasm right over the horizon, ready to devour me whole. All the pressure against both sides of my inner walls is about to drive me out of my mind completely.

J starts up again and entwines his fingers with mine, rocking back and forth slowly. It feels so amazing I feel like I'm on the verge of tears.

Adonis gives my ass a good, hard smack and speeds up as much as J has slowed down, pushing me even closer to the razor's edge of my climax.

I'm whimpering now, loud and desperate for some kind of release.

So is Adonis. I can hear him whispering all kinds of filth in my ear, but I still only have eyes for J.

He must feel inside how close I am. He pulls down my torso to meet his as Adonis keeps pummeling me from behind, and the severe change in the angle combined with the searing kiss J lays on me makes me implode.

I come so hard I scream my throat raw and black out for a couple of seconds, my entire body convulsing with the force of it. I'm still shivering and shaking with aftershocks when I come back to myself after God knows how long. I don't even remember changing positions. By the time my soul rejoins my body, Adonis is standing next to Darren as they both hover with fisted members over Claudine, who is now on her knees before them as if awaiting the blessing of their sperm on her face.

Blinking my bleary eyes, I turn my head back to find J standing over me in a similar position. His handsome face looks taut and tense as he strokes himself and studies me.

I feel like he knew the instant the idea of joining Claudine on the floor to share in the bounty of manhood that was coming to her crossed my mind.

J pumps his hand faster, swirling it around his tip with a low grunt before returning to the shaft. "I want you to take only my cum tonight," he says, his voice rough with the strain of maintaining control.

Yeah, he knew. But the rapturous expression of destruction descending upon his face makes me put a hand between my legs to rub myself and reach out weakly with the other to stroke his tight balls. "You can come wherever you want, daddy."

That does it. With a roar like a wild animal, J's cock erupts with the largest load I've ever seen from him, spurt after spurt of thick, creamy fluid landing between my breasts and across my stomach.

About two seconds later, Darren and Adonis shoot off as well, one after the other, until the room is filled with the delirious cries of the satisfied male.

I can feel J trembling when he bends down low to kiss me again, and I wrap my arms and legs around his neck and torso and hold him tight to my body. This is all I wanted. He's okay, *we're* okay, and I had my fun as well. The hope I feel at being able to have J and my BDSM life is almost as good as the orgasm.

I'm not sure how I make it out of the viewing room on my own two feet. My legs are still shaking so hard I can barely keep myself upright, let alone walk down the hall and up the stairs under my own power.

J and I both suck in deep pulls of air heavily laced with the scents of sex for a long time afterward, neither of us able to roll off the bed. Even once we're breathing normally again, J moves slower than I've ever seen when he finally gets up and starts getting ready to leave the room.

A giggling Claudine sees me struggle to peel myself off the mattress in my post-orgasmic stupor after J has had his way with me and pulls both my arms to help me stand, throwing one of her personal, embroidered silk robes around my body and ushering me to the ladies' sitting room down the hall.

I think the room served the same purpose in the mansion's original inhabitants. The wallpaper has been modernized and a wall of enameled lockers have been added since then, but the fancy crown molding and enormous mosaic tiled fireplace remain. It also smells faintly of crushed rose petals in here, which I always appreciate.

"I see why you like him so much," Claudine says with a conspiratorial wink, handing me a moist towel from one of the warmers so I can… wipe up. "I've seen him around before but never had the pleasure. He almost made me slip a disc."

Wait, who…. oh. My brain is still a little fuzzy, but a deep chuckle rattles in my chest when I realize she's referring to J's prowess in the bedroom department. That's the extent of the noise I make by way of response. I'm too exhausted for anything more than that. Even dragging this rapidly cooling towel over my skin feels like a herculean task.

I collapse more than sit on one of the nearby oversized chaise lounges. I shake my head, still not fully back on earth. "He was actually in rare form tonight. I've never seen him quite like…" I pause, blinking while I try to think of words to describe the level J had been on tonight and coming up with nothing. "Like *that*."

Claudine hums appreciatively and begins retrieving her street clothes from the locker she'd selected earlier in the evening. I guess she was out for the count, too. "Well, the entire night was delightful. I'm glad he decided to come along. You bring him with you any time you want to play, okay?"

Dressed now, she grins at me as she puts her diamond studs back into her ears.

Her devilish smile always makes me laugh. "Yes, ma'am."

I hand back her robe so she can tuck it away and give her a hug. She squeezes me back and then gives me a quick, chaste kiss on the lips.

"See you next time, kiddo," Claudine says, strutting away and leaving me to don my coat and find my way back to my man on my own.

I'm in desperate need of food and an energy drink, not to mention starting to become so sore between my legs I'm walking funny, but I manage to make my way back upstairs to the main gathering area. This time of night there's barely anyone who wasn't already downstairs or gone home, so I easily spot J standing near the entrance, waiting for me.

His eyes gleam when he sees me. He doesn't say a word when I sail into his arms as if my feet never touched the ground. He kisses me deeply and tucks me under his arm so I can lean into him.

I have no idea what time it is, but the sky is dark as pitch and there's slightly less people roaming the streets, so we are definitely in wee-hour territory.

J and I walk to the curb and wait for a cab. The night is misty and cold, making me regret wearing only my thin trench coat over my skimpy outfit. My legs are bare and I'm shivering within minutes. J turns my body toward him fully and I relish in the opportunity to share his body heat. Feeling all that firm muscle beneath his shirt doesn't hurt, either.

J is still quiet, but at least now, it feels contemplative instead of tense and full of unspoken angst. I can deal with that. I lift my chin to stare at his profile in the amber light of the streetlamp over our heads. The strong jaw, the prominent cheekbones, the full lips and long lashes… I have to suppress a sigh. I've never seen a man so beautiful in my life. I'll never get over it.

J catches me ogling and smirks. Then, in keeping with his new and improved mood, he lifts my chin higher with a hooked finger and kisses me like I'm a new bride.

My heart… Jesus, it starts beating so fast in my throat it makes me lightheaded. His lips tease and coax mine to comply and I give in with a willing eagerness that startles even myself after everything my body has been through tonight. I want him again already. I want to feel him wedged so deep inside me I can't move. I'm not sure I can physically handle it in my current state, but the desire is there and sharp as broken glass all the same.

We're still kissing when a cab finally pulls up, breaking apart just long enough for each of us to slide into the back seat before our lips are attached to each other again. I feel giddy, like a horny teenager who finally bagged the guy that every girl in the school has always wanted, and he wants me just as badly. His hands are everywhere – sliding into my coat to squeeze my waist, drifting over my breasts and hardened nipples, stroking the column of my throat. He doesn't drift lower the way I expect him to, and that only makes the newly reestablished ache there grow more intense. I'm ready to let him take me in the back seat of this cab like a drunk midnight hookup.

J's laughter is low and hungry in my ear before he speaks. "It's so late already… do you want to come to my place for the night?"

As if he really had to ask.

I throw myself back into our kiss, slipping him a little more tongue for emphasis, groaning low in my throat at all the sin I still taste on him.

J pulls away a fraction to nip at my bottom lip, already puffy again from the friction we've created between us once more. "I'll take that as a yes."

His eyes are laughing. This playful side of him is going to be my downfall. I don't think I'm capable of telling him no when he's like this. "Yes! Obviously. Absolutely."

He falls against my lips again, this time treating my upper thighs to some firm strokes that get my blood and heart pumping harder in anticipation of what's to come. I feel so… young. Desirable. Wanted. It's an addictive elixir and I can't get enough of it. I can't get enough of *him*.

CHAPTER

Three

The new bout of nerves doesn't truly kick in until I come up for air and realize we've made it to his apartment. It's been a long while since we've been together in his space, long enough for things to potentially be awkward away from the heightened sexual energy of the BDSM club. Here it'll be just J and me, alone. If things were to go sideways at any point, he has home field advantage.

That thought simmers on low heat in the back of my mind as he helps me out of the cab, pays the driver, then takes my hand so we can head inside.

After the long ride up the elevator, I find myself praying when he puts his keys in the lock and opens the door.

Please, let nothing be different than earlier tonight.

Let him stay open with me, exactly like this.

Please don't let either of us say something stupid and ruin the remainder of a beautiful night.

J clearly has no such concerns. He presses me against the front door with his body the second he closes it, lips scorching my neck with kisses that promise a return to the heaven he showed me earlier in the night.

This time, however, the longer we devour each other, the more my anxiety grows. Part of me is waiting for the other shoe to drop when it comes to J's new attitude. Everything about this is still so new, and there hasn't been nearly enough time since our encounter at the bar for him to truly show and prove his sincerity. Maybe he simply wanted to fuck me in front of the others to show his dominance. Maybe he agreed to playing with me and my little crew to save face, to protect his manhood. I don't know. I don't know anything, now that I really think about it, and the doubts are starting to eat me up from the inside out.

J backs away, startling me until I realize he's trying to take my coat from me to hang it up on the coat rack. Dazed, I hand it over.

"Why don't you get comfortable on the couch?"

He looks amused when he says it, and though I can't tell if he's poking fun at my reactions a bit, I don't have the energy or emotional bandwidth at the present moment to push him on it. I do as he suggests and plop myself down on his comfy leather couch with a grateful sigh.

J doesn't join me immediately, instead heading for the kitchen to start piddling around in the fridge. My lady bits are crying out for release, but I forget when my stomach starts grumbling loud enough for anyone sitting next to me to hear. Come to think of it, I don't think I've eaten anything since early this morning. No wonder I can barely move around after all that physical exertion.

J asks if I'm hungry and I answer before the question has fully left his lips, making him laugh.

Well, so far, so good. There hasn't been some ridiculous Jekyll and Hyde-esque transformation in him since we've arrived. I take a deep breath, forcing my body to relax as I release the air and pull my legs up so I can rest my chin on my knees and watch him.

J busies himself with slicing up a bunch of different fruits and arranging them in his artful way on a large, white plate. With the way he keeps licking the tips of his fingers as he works and triggering vivid memories of what that tongue is capable of, it doesn't take long for my sluggish energy levels to come roaring back to match my libido.

My eyes remain glued to him as I shrug off and toss aside what remains of my clothing.

Pride fills my chest when he glances up and drops the knife on the stone counter with a clink, although I'm beyond glad he didn't cut himself. I give him my sauciest smile that J returns in kind.

"You keep that up and you're going to get what you're aiming for, Gorgeous."

In the cool air of his apartment, my skin tingles all over, and the sense of power I felt at the club returns along with the sense of floating effervescence. I feel like I've been drinking all night.

I lean back along the length of the couch and prop myself up on its arm in my totally nude state, spreading my legs as wide as they will go.

I stare at him and say, "Maybe that's exactly what I want." Even from this distance, I can tell his eyes have caught the gleam of the overhead, recessed lights on my wetness. It's like my body instantly lubes up in his presence no matter how innocuous the activity we're engaged in.

Plate in hand, J stalks his way over and sets it down on the spotless coffee table, never tearing his gaze from mine. My mouth goes dry when he disrobes and discards the rest of his clothes until he is as beautifully naked as me. His smooth skin has the same rich color and luster as roasted coffee beans, and all I want to do is rub myself all over his body.

How do I never tire of seeing him like this?

He settles himself on the coffee table near the plate instead of on the couch with me. I don't like that, so I decide to punish him with a little display and fondle the juncture of my thighs, pulling my fingers away from my hot flesh again and again so he can see the trails of my stickiness suspended in the air.

My clit is already tingly and plump and sensitive from the overstimulation of the night, so I already know I'm not going to last long if I keep it up. I'm still too weak for the willpower required to keep an orgasm at bay for any significant length of time.

J quickly tires of my games. He reaches out and grabs my wrist, stilling me, before leaning forward to slowly suck my wet fingers clean before my eyes.

His tongue slicks out to gather every last drop and I am utterly lost.

When he's finished, he plucks a chunk of pineapple from the plate before placing it between my parted lips. It lands on my tongue in an explosion of sweet, tangy flavor, and I make a big show of chewing slowly and swallowing and licking my lips to let him know how much I enjoyed it.

"Very good," J says, making my stomach do a flip when he leans down again to kiss me, tasting as much of my mouth as he can to vicariously relive my experience with the tropical fruit. My eyes close and I can barely feel my body. This is amazing… more sensuality from him than I even knew he was capable of. Our tongues entwine and tease each other, languid and unhurried, and his moans of pleasure become louder than mine.

He retreats only to get another piece of fruit, and I realize he is truly reveling in this as much as I am. We repeat the process over and over: J feeding me, J tasting me. Once he gets to the blood oranges, they're so juicy that things start to get messy, their sweetness leaking past my lips and dripping down my chin and neck onto my chest. J doesn't miss a beat, chasing each drop of decadence with tongue and lips until I am writhing against the couch cushions, the leather making sucking sounds against my backside as I move.

Sexuality always seemed to come easily to J since we met – it was via a BDSM dating app, after all – but this felt… different. This felt intimate in a way we never were before.

J's eyes are like dark fire as he moves to position himself lower on the couch, until his pelvis is hovering directly over mine.

I hope he isn't gentle.

He isn't.

J hooks his elbows beneath my thighs and buries himself to the hilt with one mighty surge of his hips that briefly makes a shout – and my soul – leave my body.

I'm already panting and clawing at his back when he slowly and mercilessly retreats, returning to give me short, shallow strokes that do nothing but feed my maddening, aching need for every part of him.

He wants to torture me. I don't know why but he must, because why else would he move so tortuously slow when my hips are bucking so fast beneath the heavy press of his bodyweight they're practically vibrating?

My chest heaves against his, sweat making our skin slippery. "Please…" I don't want to beg and sound as pathetic as I feel right now, but I can't seem to help it.

J ignores me, pressing my knees up near my head to keep me from moving around so much, and takes to pushing himself in and out of my opening a mere few inches, the pressure and his erratic pace driving me out of my mind.

He's taken control from me and I feel a sense of relief. I let him have it, relinquishing every last trace of tension in my body from the deepest parts of my psyche that fear becoming fully vulnerable.

I'm completely at his mercy.

This feels totally different than the trust required when handcuffs or the X-rack are involved. With every slow push and pull of J's body inside of mine, I feel him tear another layer of emotional armor away, until all that remains is a quivering mess of a woman and all I can think is *I love him… I love him… I love him.*

I am laid bare in every possible way.

A shift in J's expression lets me know he sees it, and I feel him harden even more against my inner walls, thickening to the point he can barely move.

And with the way he's looking down at me, staring into my eyes like he can see everything I ever was and can ever be...

Moisture gathers in my lashes and my vision of him gets a little blurry. My voice comes out a delirious rasp. "I… I'm gonna come…"

J instantly stops moving and I nearly burst into real tears. "What… why did you –"

"Not yet." J's entire body is quaking against mine, his lips trembling against my lips. "Wait… wait for me…"

"Oh, Jesus…"

I can't hold on anymore. I can't. The vibrations from J's low, continuous groan in my ear I can feel in my chest. I can no longer separate his breath from mine in my throat. He feels even more a part of me than he had earlier tonight at the club, which I didn't think was possible.

This. This had to be the elusive kind of intimacy I had always craved but could never name because I'd never seen it. Truly making love because there's a real emotional connection between us. A shared experience. A mutual vulnerability.

It's glorious.

"I meant what I said at the bar, Brooklyn."

J's quiet admission takes me off guard, clearing my lust-blurred vision as I focus on him. "I believe you." I'm so hoarse from all the panting, I barely recognize my own voice.

"But you never gave me an answer."

I didn't?

My mind rolls through flashing images of earlier in the night, which now feels like it happened a long time ago. My stomach turns when I realize he's right. I dragged him off with Claudine and the guys before we'd really finished our conversation. I feel bad about leaving him hanging like that.

"Well? Is that what you want, too?"

I don't even have to think about it. We're having a full-blown discussion about the state of our relationship with our genitals linked and it feels like the most natural thing in the world.

This is exactly where I'm supposed to be.

"Yeah," I say, a grin stretching across my flushed face. "I want this with you. I want to try."

Happiness looks so good on him. He gives me the sweetest lop-sided smile and returns to his shallow, even stroke, making my heart do a strange flutter behind my ribs. I can tell he really does want this — want *us*.

Especially when J starts leaving the softest kisses over every inch of my overheated skin that his mouth can reach — each eyelid, the tips of my ears, the hollow of my neck. All I can do is shake with the force of the climax roiling to the surface. I can't keep my thoughts together a second longer.

"Come on." J's voice sounds strained, barely under control. That's all he says and I instinctively know what he means. He's finally picked up the pace and it's one thrust, then two, and then –

Pleasure of a magnitude I've never felt hits low and heavy and hot in my belly. My entire body seizes up at the same exact moment that I feel J's solid thickness jerk rhythmically against my tightening muscles. He moans like an injured man against my neck while I cry out as if the entire world is crashing down around us, and I don't think I've ever been this happy in my life.

I wake up in bed with a gasp so ragged it makes me cough, my eyes scanning the room in confusion. This doesn't look like my bedroom.

Oh. Oh, yeah. I stretch like a satisfied cat and cover my body back up with the pure white sheet. This is J's bed.

I can't remember the last time I slept that hard. No dreams or anything, just dead to the world for who knows how many hours. The sun is streaming in great swaths across the wooden floor, so it could be early afternoon already. Come to think of it, I'm not even sure how I made it to the bed. Did J carry me in here?

Where is he, anyway?

"J?" I sit up again, pausing to listen for any sounds of movement in the bathroom or on the other side of the closed bedroom door in the hallway. "J! Are you out there?"

I wait for way longer than necessary, unable to stem the tide of disappointment washing over me. After our incredible night, how could he not be here when I woke up?

His absence throws a bucket of ice water all over my remaining euphoria. I might have misread him last night. Or perhaps I misread myself.

On the bright side, at least it's Sunday and work can wait another day. I need some time to sort through all these emotions. I'm going to need it if J is having second thoughts.

Chewing on my lip to battle the onslaught of anxiety, I look around for my phone and find it neatly plugged into a charger on the nightstand. I couldn't have done it. A blush heats my face and neck at J taking care of me while I was out like a light, even in such a small way. But that only makes his disappearance more confusing, not less.

I tap the screen on my cell. Only one missed call, this one from Sherry. She and I have become close since I spilled my guts to her about the shame I felt over my secret BDSM life a few months ago. Since then, she's become my biggest fan and a wonderful friend to me.

When I start to call her on pure instinct alone, I find myself hesitating. I should probably work out how I feel about my situation before I muddy the waters trying to talk things through with my friend. Or better yet, talk it over with J. If he ever intends to come back today.

I'm halfway done writing a text to Sherry to tell her I'd call her back later when the door opens, startling me out of my skin.

My entire being smiles when I see J striding into the room with a tray full of food and I instantly start giggling. "What's all that?"

"Breakfast. Or brunch, as it were." I've never seen J smile quite this much, and I have to say I like it tremendously. "Since you were so exhausted and I was certainly too tired to cook anything, I went out to that bagel spot you love so much." He sits the tray on the bed next to me with a flourish.

There he goes, taking care of me again. My face heats again and I hide it by crossing my arms over my bent knees and placing my cheek on my wrist. "Thank you. It smells amazing."

"It was all I could do not to tear into one before I made it back. I'm starving." Evidently tired of waiting, J grabs a plain bagel from the tray and takes a huge, chewy bite, no smear or anything.

I'm not quite so uncivilized, so I daintily spread some of the cream cheese he brought on half of one of my favorite multigrain bagels, despite the fact that my hand is trembling. It's been so long since I've eaten, my blood sugar levels are probably in the basement.

Speaking of civility…I realize when I go to take a bite that I'm still assed-out under the covers. I can at least put a shirt on so I don't get crumbs all over my breasts.

J's hand on my knee stops my momentum. "Don't get up. I like you like this, au naturel in the sunlight." He ducks his head when he says it, like it was embarrassing for him to admit. The tiny gesture nearly makes my heart pop.

So, I tuck my wild hair behind my ear and take that bite of my sinfully delicious bagel. God, best in the borough.

J gets up to throw the curtains aside and let more light in before he returns to the bed at my side. The city streets many floors below us are filled with everyday chaos, but J and I sit together in our own private haven in silence.

I can feel him, and seeing the look of contentment on his face, he can clearly feel me, too. No words needed.

CHAPTER

Four

I can't get over it. I feel like my entire body has been buzzing for weeks. J has been so open with me lately, in a way he never was before we made our situation official. Sort of. Fine, maybe not in a way that actually tells me anything concrete about his past – details about which I'm still salivating for – but it *is* different between us, and for that reason, I'm willing to be patient. It's already paying off. Even if his mouth has been pretty quiet, J's body has been telling me things I haven't heard from him before, and not only when we're whiling away hours between the sheets.

I've noticed it during the in-between times, when I'm helping him do laundry at his place or he's helping me prepare a meal at mine. The way his hand lingers on my naked shoulder after a squeeze. How his lips and tongue have become so soft and teasing with mine, like he wants to savor every nuance of the way I taste whenever we take the time to lose ourselves in a kiss. Everything is slower, more tender. It's intoxicating. I don't think I'll ever get enough of it –

"Brooklyn, are you trying to scrape a hole through the bottom of my pot?"

"Huh?" Blinking, I come back to myself and turn to look at my mother, who is staring at me with wide eyes and raised eyebrows. With her hand on her hip, she strikes such a similar figure to the version of her I remember doling out punishment in my youth, I'm a little taken aback.

She chuckles instead of giving me a smack. "You've been stirring in the same spot for the last twenty minutes. It's spaghetti, okay? We're not making a roux for gumbo."

I roll my eyes at myself, cheeks heating from a bit of embarrassment. Hard to believe I'm here daydreaming like a teen in love for the first time, but what can I do? I hardly have my head on straight anymore and I know it.

I put the spoon down on the counter, on my mom's ceramic spoon rest that's fashioned like a grinning frog. It's hideous, but she loves that kind of stuff. "Sorry, Ma…I guess I have a lot of stuff on my mind." She doesn't know the half of it.

"I'll bet you do." Uh oh. I catch that distinct sparkle in my mother's eyes, a tell-tale sign that an interrogation was on the way, and have to suppress a groan. "What man has you all tied up in knots?" Her gaze is warm but that smile is downright devilish.

My mouth opens and I almost allow myself to gush about J and this new space we've entered in our relationship. Like it'll make things more real if I say it out loud to someone else, someone I love. Then I'll know it's not all in my head.

Something makes me reach for the tongs to fiddle with the pot containing the boiling pasta instead. "What makes you think a man has to do with anything?"

"That sex glow you got going on over there – "

"Mama!" I almost give myself whiplash spinning around to stare at her in scandalized shock. "Aside from the fact that you shouldn't know anything about that, you don't see anything of the kind – stop it." But… she's right; it's true. I swear, it's as if my happiness has become some kind of natural retinoid that has smoothed my skin and made me look ten years younger. People pay big bucks to buy the bottled version of what I've been sporting naturally for weeks.

Some strange protective feeling wells up in me out of nowhere and I bite my lip instead of spilling my guts. I tell my mother about J – and then what? She's going to ask about how I met him and where, and I'll have to tell her, and then I'll have to defend myself and him and our choices…

God. I'm exhausted just thinking about it. I can feel myself deflating already, and I want to float on air for as long as I can.

So, I shrug and echo my own thoughts aloud instead. "Have you ever considered the fact that I might be happy with my life choices?"

When my mother huffs and crosses her arms, the fringe on her velvet dressing gown does a little dance. "I'm sure you are, Tink. Doesn't mean I don't know for a fact there isn't more to it. Don't get smart."

I'm probably tiptoeing into dangerous territory with my intuitive mother; if I resist her gentle interrogation any more than I already have, I run the risk of pissing her off for real. Dangerous, especially when for her, the prospect of grandchildren is on the line.

I lower my head so I can breathe in the savory aroma of stewed tomatoes, onions and herbs rising from the steaming pot. "Smells *so good*. Didn't Grandma give you this recipe?"

The distant *bang* from the front door hitting the wall makes both of us jump.

"We're home, Mama!"

When the brilliant smile Mom seems to reserve for her only son appears, I realize I'm off the hook for now. "Is that you, Derrick?"

Of course, she knows she wasn't expecting anyone else, but this is part of the little game they like to play whenever he shows up late, which is often. Most of the time it's annoying, but tonight I'm beyond grateful for my little brother's antics.

"Yes, your favorite child has arrived," he calls from the long hallway. I hear the door close and shut out the honking horns and loud conversations of the borough street, just before Derrick yelps in pain. "Ow!"

I giggle, knowing my sister must be with him and caught him in the ribs with her elbow for that remark. "Fine – your second favorite caught a ride with me, too."

As I grab the dining ware Mom set out on the counter earlier in the evening, I throw him a playful glare when he strolls into the kitchen with my sister right behind him. Unsurprisingly, he's wearing the typical uniform of the local college student: ripped jeans he probably hasn't washed in weeks, dirty white high-top sneakers well past their prime, and a t-shirt full of moth holes. The way he struts around here, you would think Derrick wears custom three-piece suits every day.

"I'll have you know the oldest is always the favorite," I say, waggling the empty shallow bowl in my hand at him.

I offer my cheek and Derrick plants a quick peck on it before making for the kitchen table. "Sorry to tell you, sis, but that is a disgusting myth. Don't believe everything you hear."

He says it with such a deadpan expression, I can't help but laugh aloud. Such a smartass.

When I turn to greet my sister, she's staring so hard at the cell phone she has in a death grip, she doesn't even look up as she shuffles her way to an empty chair.

I wave a hand in her face. "Uh…*hello,* Bianca."

"Hey, Brook." Her voice a low murmur, she slips away from my attempt at our usual hug and takes her seat. She keeps staring down at her lap, hardly blinking as she chews on the end of one of her plentiful braids.

That's not like her to be so morose; by this point after her arrival for our standing weekly family dinners, I would have lost count of how many of my sister's smiles I had personally witnessed. She also looks a little less put together than usual. I can't remember the last time I've seen her in anything but some skin-tight jeans and a crop top, let alone in a mismatching sweatpants set.

"Boy, I *know* you did not just sit down at my kitchen table and expect to eat my exquisite food without washing off the filth from the streets – get up!" My mother swats at Derrick with a kitchen towel and practically chases him into the guest bathroom in mock outrage, him laughing and trying to dodge her the whole time.

I can't even respond to their silliness right now. My chest tightens as I watch Bianca.

After waiting until our mother's back is turned when she goes to the fridge for the iced tea she made earlier, I level a penetrating stare at my sister. "Hey," I say, making an effort to keep my voice low so as not to embarrass her in front of Mom by asking, "are you okay?"

She spares me a glance. Her dark eyes, exact copies of our mother's, have taken on a haunted look I've never seen. Not even during finals week at her university. She looks like she hasn't slept well in a long while.

"I'm fine," she says, voice flat and lifeless as a mountain lake, and she's back on her phone a second later.

There's no time to question her further because the chocolate whirlwind that is my brother is back at the table and begging for a plate, batting his long lashes at me. I roll my eyes right on cue and hand him a full dish.

I fill two more for my mom and sister, then a final one for myself before we all sit down. But not before Mom puts some vinyl on the record player sitting on its fancy gold stand near the window, of course. She did it late today since she was too busy hounding me about my love life while I was working the stove.

We all dig in, and all I hear is my brother's loud chewing and the incessant clinking of silverware.

Then Derrick makes a show of clearing his throat. "Ma, did you make this spaghetti or did your spawn?"

My hand rips off a chunk of breadstick and I toss it at him before I realize I even moved. It bounces off his forehead and falls into his plate, making my mother and I burst out laughing. "This meal was made by my own fine hands, thank you very much," I say.

Derrick shrugs, grinning as he pops my bread piece into his mouth and keeps shoveling in spaghetti without missing a beat. "Not bad for an amateur."

I chuckle. "I'll take it."

My sister's silence continues to create a joy vacuum at the table and my eyes slide over to where she sits next to Derrick, across the table from my mother and I. My brother is too involved in his meal to pay attention to such things. Mom noticed also, but she knows Bianca will balk if my mother tries to call out an issue. My sister is flighty like that. You have to talk *around* issues with Bianca, circling closer and closer until she feels comfortable enough to finally reveal what has her so troubled. At least, that's how she used to be when she was younger.

Damn…come to think of it, when was the last time we had a conversation like that? When she was fresh out of high school, maybe?

I am definitely slacking in the big sister department.

While I mull over the best way to approach Bianca without triggering the most negative response possible, Derrick easily fills in the quiet with some funny story about a prank he pulled on a kid who was sleeping in the middle of one of his lectures. He has an endless supply of tales like these and they never fail to entertain. But while my mother yuks it up with him, I can't pull my attention from Bianca and the dark cloud she's dragged in with her tonight.

"Bianca, what did you think of my sauce? I know you like yours tangy over sweet, like I do – "

"It's fine. I'm not really hungry." Bianca stares at her food as she pushes her saucy noodles around her plate. Apparently true to her word, she's barely eaten any of it, but at least she's off her phone for the moment.

Biting my lip, I notice the worry I feel settling deeper into my chest, and I don't like it at all. But I have to be careful. She's a young woman barely into her twenties who hates being questioned about anything. She was hard headed as a kid and it's only gotten more pronounced as she's aged.

Okay, let me try something else…

"You have a big lunch on campus today or something? And how are your classes going?" My question almost aborts on its own with the realization that I don't even know what classes she's taking right now. Or her major. To be fair, she's already changed it at least twice, but still.

As her big sister, I should know *something* up to date about her life, shouldn't I?

"No." Bianca runs a fingertip over each of her eyebrows to smooth them and of course, her phone is back in her hand again the moment I blinked. "And my classes are – "

"Fine, yeah. I get it," I finish for her, deflating and sitting back in my chair. Derrick gives me a strange look but keeps telling mom about the rebuild of some hotrod he's been working on with a friend for months.

Now it's my turn to pick at my food since my appetite has long gone. I surreptitiously glance at Bianca as if seeing her for the first time, my stomach slowly twisting into a surprising knot as I try to think back to the last time that I've had a substantive conversation with my sister, on the phone or in person.

I can't remember. And the kernel of truth buried deep inside that realization, the one that's triggered the creeping chill down my back, makes me feel like a piece of shit.

Bianca is clearly going through something and is doing a horrible job at hiding it. I've been so caught up in my own life, trying to figure out what I want and how to get it, that I've let my family fall by the wayside. Maybe I've been so used to the high functionality of our little family, with so little drama and trauma for the most part, that I've taken it for granted. Very little ever seems to shake my brother's confidence, so I've only ever worried about him getting a girl pregnant before he was ready. Mom kind of floats through a universe of her own making most of the time, so she's usually the one checking in on us.

Bianca was a happy-go-lucky kind of kid who grew a little more reserved as she got older, but it was still easy to make her laugh. I don't know this version of my sister sitting across from me, and I'm sure my general selfishness is the reason that's ninety percent my fault.

Before I can start wallowing in self-pity, however, my mom nudges my arm. "Did you hear what I said?"

"No, sorry," I say, my hand drifting up to rub at the back of my neck, my face and chest heating uncomfortably. "What did you say?"

"I was telling your brother you said you were going to tell me about this man-friend of yours that has you all…glowy."

I choke on my sip of iced tea. "Excuse me? I told you no such thing, mother." If I'm being honest, I love J to death but thinking about him right now with my sister so close by makes me feel guilty beyond belief.

"You know she got that lying habit from your father," Mom says to my brother, who gives her a sage nod in agreement.

"Okay, stop," I say as they both laugh, sensing the turn in conversation is about to get out of control. I look deeply into my mother's smiling eyes. "Mom, I have a man. Yes, he is good to me. No, I don't want to talk about it. Okay?"

She looks disappointed enough to cry, and the image is so absurd I burst out laughing. "Really, Tink? That's all I get? I'm on the cusp of grandmotherhood and you won't tell me anything?"

I give her a deep, long-suffering sigh. "It's new and I don't want to jinx it."

"Aw, leave her alone, Ma," Derrick says with an innocent grin, raising my eyebrows. "If she wants to ruin that man's life in peace, let her do her thing."

I stick my tongue out at him instead of thanking him for sticking up for me like I started to. "Shut up, D." Of course, he only laughs like he's told the world's greatest joke.

Having had my eye on her during my entire exchange with the other members of my family, Bianca hasn't so much as cracked a smile the whole time. Part of me wants to try to engage her again, but…it's probably better if I don't for now.

When we finish up dinner, some scary movie, and my mother and brother have finished with the dishes, I trot through the living room to catch up with Bianca at the front door before she can head outside to wait at Derrick's car.

"Hey…Bianca, wait a minute."

She looks downright exasperated when she finally turns and looks up at me, but I try not to let it deter me despite the sudden lump that's appeared in my throat. Why the hell am I nervous?

I can't overthink this. I grab my sister and pull her into a tight hug before she has time to figure out what's going on. I can't remember the last time I was so intentional about this either, but I can't dwell on it.

The annoyance on her face has morphed into genuine surprise by the time I let her go. Honestly, that's more painful than I expected it to be. "Listen," I say, looking at her and trying not to stare at the distinct grayness of caramel complexion that's concentrated beneath each of her eyes. "If there's something going on, something that's not…all that great, you can tell me. Okay?"

Her surprise vanishes the instant the words leave my mouth, replaced with something that looks so similar to contempt, I take a step back on instinct. "Since when?" she says, and her sharp reply feels like razor wire in my heart.

I…I don't even know what to say to that. My mouth opens and closes a few times and I'm sure I look like a dying fish, but she's gutted me with two words. She's never talked to me like that with any real sense of discord between us, and it's even worse because I had no idea it was there at all.

How long has she hated me like this?

I don't get to ask. Hearing our brother saying goodbye to Mom and looking past me to see him bound down the concrete steps to the sidewalk, Bianca rolls her eyes and jumps into the front passenger seat the moment the chirp from his key fob announces the door locks have disengaged.

Backing away from the curb, I barely feel the one-armed hug Derrick slings over my shoulder before he makes for the driver's door. I suddenly want to cry so badly. I have to find a way to fix this.

From the moment the elevator doors slide open onto my floor at work, my life immediately replaces the source of one intense anxiety – my brooding little sister with the mysterious issues – for the one I've been suffering through every weekday for months now. The only thing that gets me through it is the knowledge that my assistant and I have perfected all the ways of avoiding each other during the day down to an art.

Without any prior discussion, one day we started taking lunches at slightly different times, until she was heading out a full half hour before or after I did. We began sitting several seats apart at weekly staff meetings, earning more than a few curious glances from my colleagues and their support staff. It has even come to the point where Nikki was usually – and conveniently – assisting one of the other producers on our floor at any given moment during the day instead of hovering like a curious bee in my office with me, the way she used to in the not-so-distant past.

Ironically, the drastic change reminds me why I hired Nikki in the first place; we instantly operated on the same wavelength with no clear effort on our parts. Like we had an unspoken language between the two of us only we understood. Even when we didn't necessarily want to see or speak to each other.

After J's encouragement to face my fear and loathing of intense awkwardness, I'd had a little chat with Nikki in the stairwell a while back about each of us being comfortable with owning our sexuality and not being ashamed, blah blah blah. I suppose neither of us could take it to heart in the end. She fled from that dank stairwell like her hair was on fire and I've barely seen her since. I was and am still embarrassed to the core about every single minute that transpired between us, and with the way Nikki has fallen right in line with my own behavior, I know she still has to be mortified, too.

Regardless of the hoops we continue to jump through on a daily basis to save face, Nikki and I are both utmost professionals and still get done what we need to somehow. My desk has become the central hub for our nonverbal communication efforts, with countless exchanges of memos and sticky notes and emails throughout the day. I don't think I've ever written or typed so much for this specific purpose in this job, but I won't dare complain if it keeps me from thinking about how my production assistant knows what I sound like when I come each and every time I see her face.

My eyes are adept at avoiding eye contact with Nikki at this point as I walk down the hall to the glass-walled conference room in the center of this floor within our multistory building. I know she's there, but I've learned to block her from my peripheral vision. For no reason I can claim, the clicking of my own high heels on the freshly buffed tile floor spikes my anxiety further.

We have a near miss when I snatch a Danish from the assortment Nikki is in the process of arranging on a large tray in the middle of the long conference table. My heart drops to my shoes the instant before I realize our skin hasn't actually touched. I hurry to my seat – as far away from Nikki's on the other end as possible – and do my best to stay awake for this budget meeting, the first of the new fiscal quarter.

This turns out to be far less difficult than I anticipate after I find I have to engage in more than one verbal tussle, as what is usually a very dry discussion turns into a heated debate. Several of the other daytime producers mistakenly believe they deserve a larger cut of the overall budget for the month than any other department, and I have to put them in line before their demands get out of hand completely. Considering the amount of stress I'm under has turned the muscles in my back to solid concrete, I'm not sure how I manage to keep my cool. But I do, and I'm out of there quickly and into the break room so I can catch my breath – and quell my overwhelming urge to smack everyone who showed up for the meeting for being stupid.

Ugh. The audacity! Trying to hijack the budget I have slaved over for weeks! I was the one who volunteered to take it on when no one else would do it, and yes, I was selfishly thinking I could ensure the shows in my line up would get the financial support they've been begging me for. I hand my colleagues a virtually perfect budget proposal and they try to snatch it from me.

I'm still so hot as fish grease about it that I can feel the sweat gathering on my forehead and threatening to ruin my makeup. My violet blazer feels stifling. I shrug out of it and toss it onto the nearest chair as I turn to make for the coffee pot and some modicum of stress relief – and find Nikki already there, standing at the counter.

And *shit* – she's locked eyes with me already. I'll look like a neurotic idiot if I do the about-face my entire body is screaming for me to do and flee the room entirely.

I also can't stand here frozen like an idiot popsicle, half in the room and half in the hallway.

Okay, why am *I* the one tempted to run away here? I'm still the boss at the end of the day, even if I've made some decisions in my recent past that have left me exposed in a way I don't think I'll ever feel comfortable with again…I'm still allowed to be human, right?

My spine straightening after my little self-pep talk, I practically march to my intended destination by the sink. Nikki is still hanging around, so she must have just had a similar conversation with herself.

I offer my usual tight half-smile on the off chance she's looking my way, but I don't try to confirm that's the case. Instead, I reach into the glass-paneled cupboard for my favorite coffee mug and try not to chew my own lip off from the tension. I can barely breathe as it is.

Nikki doesn't speak. Neither do I. The sound of the coffee I pour into my mug is louder than whatever it is playing on the radio sitting on a nearby table and grates on my already frayed nerves. I hope – pray – she doesn't notice the way my hand holding the pot is trembling.

When I take a sip from my mug, I gag as the acrid flavor of black coffee hits the back of my tongue. I was so distracted I didn't even get my usual cream and two sugars. Ugh.

Nikki still hasn't moved, and now I'm starting to wonder why she hasn't run for the hills yet. We're alone in a room even smaller than one of the viewing rooms at the BDSM club; my close proximity alone should have her ready to jump out of her skin if she's feeling anything like I am right now.

My eyes flick to my right. That's when I notice Nikki has been washing and rewashing her own coffee cup in the small stainless-steel sink. Probably has been since I walked in here.

Strangely, watching her makes me feel a tiny bit better. It's solid evidence I'm not the only one who is losing her mind and tired of it.

We've created a toxic work environment between the two of us with the rest of the staff in this building none the wiser. And God knows we can't go to human resources for any solutions.

Maybe I should try to broach the subject again with her. I've been lying to myself all this time, believing that continuing to operate like this in my place of business is actually sustainable.

When I open my mouth to say something– and honestly, who knows what that's going to be – the song playing on the radio changes and my attention automatically clicks in. I've heard it before, some smooth jazz piece that seems like it should be playing in a hotel lobby or the elevator in a corporate building like this one.

I normally don't pay much attention to the radio in general, but something about it makes the hairs on the back of my neck stand straight up and a chill skitters under my skin. Why does it sound so familiar?

I squint, I'm trying so hard to listen closely…and oh, God…the club.

This is the exact song that was playing through the built-in speakers in the viewing room when Nikki first had her face buried between my legs, before I opened my big rambling mouth and accidentally revealed the true reality of our connection.

The vision of her encounter with J and myself is so sudden and vivid, I can feel my cheeks and chest heat like someone dashed a pot of boiling water in my face. Actually, that scenario would probably be more enjoyable than this moment.

While I swallow convulsively and try to compose myself like an adult with actual control of her emotions, I continue to give Nikki the side eye. Had she heard it, too? Beyond putting her now squeaky-clean cup back in the cupboard and then bracing both hands on the edge of the granite counter, she hasn't moved around much.

What is she doing? Why is she still standing here?

Suddenly, I notice her shoulders shaking, the delicate folds of her peach silk blouse shifting along with her body's subtle movements.

For the love of all that is holy…she's crying and I'm about to panic. I'm too raw and in my own feelings right now to handle this.

But then, Nikki throws her head back and I realize she's *laughing*.

Laughing!

My brain can't keep up with this emotional rollercoaster and I stare at her blankly until she finally stops.

The laughter must have acted as some kind of catharsis; Nikki looks calmer and more clear-eyed than I've seen her in a long time. She dares to meet my eyes. "What are the odds, right?"

She heard the song, all right. She giggles this time, presumably at the shock that has my face frozen in place.

It takes a long moment for her smile to loosen me up enough to recall human speech, but I finally say, "You could say that about our entire situation outside of this office."

Nikki blinks at me, and I worry that my response came out angry when it sounded like lighthearted banter in my head until she rolls her eyes. "Truer words have never been spoken," she says, shaking her head. She turns around to head deeper into the room at last. We were probably standing together at the sink for only a few seconds, but with all the emotions I've experienced, it feels like years.

"Feel like sitting for a second?"

This time it's my turn to blink like a startled bunny. "Oh, uh…sure." I take my dramatically bitter coffee and follow her to the round table of her choice. There are four empty chairs, and for reasons I can't begin to understand, I settle myself in the one right next to hers. Maybe the sudden break in the tension between us has me feeling super social. I know for certain the absence of it relaxed my shoulders and back in a way that even J's skilled hands haven't been able to recently.

I decide to trust my voice – and mind – to speak in clear, cohesive sentences. "So…we haven't done this in a long time." I raise a very deliberate eyebrow at her. "Could be wrong, but it certainly seems like you've been avoiding me."

"Oh, wow," Nikki says, laughing again but closing herself off unconsciously by crossing her arms over her chest. The movement creates a bit of cleavage above her neckline, instantly reminding me of how perfect her breasts looked as they hung in my face from above –

Stop it. I am not going there.

"Honestly, Boss," Nikki continues, "I was just following your lead, your energy. I didn't – and still don't – want to cause you any issues. Here or-or…elsewhere." The look she gives me is so earnest it makes my chest ache.

We really need to talk this out. In a free and authentic way, beyond the walls of this office and its many prying eyes and ears. Speak every word we need to say with no holds barred.

Taking a breath, I close my eyes and open them once more. I need to take charge of my life again. "What would you say to grabbing some dinner after work? I think it would be good to, you know, catch up *for real*. Besides, there's nothing to eat here except stale donuts."

I am appalled by the way my heartbeat accelerates as I wait for her answer, legit terrified at the prospect of having egg on my face if my own assistant tells me to get lost because she's got better things to do on a weeknight.

Trying not to think about *who* that might entail, I bite my lip and try to keep my smile from fading into nothingness.

Nikki's smile is languid. Its unhurried arrival doing nothing to diminish its brightness, and I find myself grinning back at her like someone off their meds. "Uh, first of all, speak for yourself; stale donuts happen to be delicious after a go in the microwave. And yeah, we can do that. But only if I can pick the place." Her eyes take on a steely glint that surprises me. "I think that's fair."

A smirk tugs at my mouth. Still so saucy. I hadn't realized I had grown so accustomed to Nikki tiptoeing around this place like a church mouse for so long. I've missed this part of her personality – her quick wit and smart mouth. I'm always amazed anew at how similar we are in so many ways. Especially now that we enjoy a lot of the same, ah…*things.*

I hope the relationship we have now hasn't become so messy and complicated that the cool bond we had before is lost altogether.

If I say that, though, I run the risk of looking both thirsty and insane, so I don't. "Fine. Text me the place and I'll meet you there. Just make sure it's not trash, okay? Your taste in food sometimes…" I make a face, "it can be a little iffy."

"Ha! You wish. That last sushi and sub sandwiches place we went to changed your life; don't lie."

Just like that, Nikki and I fell back into step – or at least, back onto the same path…slightly more comfortable around each other now if not yet fully restored. After everything we've shared outside of this office, I'm not sure we can be. But maybe we can be something different. Something better. If nothing else, coming to work every day will make me feel a lot less likely to take a running leap out of the window to escape the unbearable tension.

CHAPTER

Six

If I say the rest of my workday went on without a hitch after my lunchtime conversation with my assistant, I'll only be lying a little.

I unintentionally came down so hard on my colleagues during the budget meeting that everyone gave me a wide berth for the rest of the day. But I noticed Nikki pass by my open doorway much more often than she had in recent days, and now she had even taken to waiting there for me to look up from working at my desk to throw me a wink or a wave before she moved on.

That is what drove me to distraction all the way up to the time I grabbed my purse and keys to head out for the evening.

Every time I think about my agreement to meet up with Nikki after work, I get this odd, twisty feeling in my gut that makes my heart race. Although I can't say it's entirely unpleasant.

Why am I so nervous?

Am I afraid of there potentially being more awkwardness at the uncomfortable questions that may come up that neither of us might want to answer?

Or is it something else...something I don't want to think about?

"Gorgeous, are you still there?"

I'm so distracted, J's rumbling voice on my speakerphone makes me jump.

"Sorry, I'm still here…what did you ask me?"

"Where did you say you were going tonight?"

"Oh, to have dinner with a coworker to catch up." I didn't know exactly where until just now when Nikki's text comes through with the name and address of the restaurant – and a little devilish smiley face emoji that makes my heart thump a little harder. Which I don't appreciate. At. All.

"Well, you can always come over to my place instead. It's steak night, you know." Both J's low purr and the promise of an amazing meal are tempting, but I shake my head even knowing he can't see me.

"I appreciate it, J. But I already agreed and I have to meet her there sooner rather than later." I'm only half paying attention trying to map the restaurant on my phone. At least it isn't far; I won't even have to take a cab.

"You sure you want to go in the first place?"

I frown. "Huh? Why do you ask that?"

"Your voice. You sound like you had to talk yourself into going."

J sounds so sure of his assessment of me, it makes me pause. "I actually asked her. She picked the restaurant."

"Hm."

I wait for a good long while for him to continue, then shake my head to myself again when he doesn't.

"Okay…what does that mean?" I'm starting to get a little frustrated with him as I push through the crowded sidewalk in the direction of the restaurant. Too much going on for me today for J to do his whole thing of not saying what he means. I don't have the time or emotional energy to interpret his words right now.

"Just curious as to why you sound almost nervous."

Goddamit. See, this is exactly why I initially planned on texting J to let him know I was going to be late tonight instead of calling.

"Well, I'm not," I say, hoping I can convince us both.

"Who are you meeting with, anyway?"

And there it is, the question I predicted was coming. The truth in this situation has way more implications than I feel comfortable with right now. We haven't talked about Nikki at all after our short conversation immediately after the fateful BDSM club meetup. What if J doesn't feel comfortable with me hanging out with her outside of work?

What if *I* don't?

I try to keep my sigh as quiet as possible so he can't hear it over the phone. "Just one of the younger girls from work." It isn't a lie, after all. "Listen, I'm not far from the restaurant and I want to call her and let her know I'm close. I'll call you as soon as I'm free again," I say, quickly signing off with him and cringing because J can see right through me.

I'll have to deal with him later.

As I walk, I try not to examine my words and actions during my exchange with J too closely because whenever I let myself think on it I don't like the way it makes me feel. I'm not a fan of dishonesty by omission, but I need a little time to figure this out on my own before J throws his lot in and muddies the already murky waters even further.

I arrive at the restaurant before I know it, a little place that looks distinctly like a hole-in-the-wall from the outside. The tiny entrance right off the intersection of two tiny streets is surrounded by a string of connected units that look like they were new in the 1950s, mostly populated with liquor stores and cheap clothing spots.

I raise an eyebrow as I take in my surroundings. With the trash blowing around in the breeze and the graffiti decorating every brick and concrete surface, it's pretty seedy but not necessarily unsafe.

Finally spotting the small red sign to the seafood restaurant, I slip my hand into my purse to grip my mace and tiptoe my way inside.

Both my eyebrows lift once I'm safely inside the interior, which is another world from the city streets beyond the doors.

It's all sleek and modern, steel and stone with colored glass accents. A uniformed hostess with blonde curls bounces forward to greet me. "Hello there and welcome! How many today?"

"Uh…" I glance around the huge space of dressed dining tables beyond the hostess, scanning the crowd for Nikki's distinctive shock of glossy black hair, but I don't see it anywhere. "I'm meeting one other person, but I don't think she's made it here yet."

"Not a problem…would you like to be seated at the bar with a drink while you wait?"

Tempting as hell, but something tells me I need to be as clear headed for this exchange tonight as possible. Nothing harder than a single glass of wine, I think. "No, a small table is fine. Just not near the kitchen or the restroom, please."

"Of course." The hostess smiles at me again, so hard her eyes crinkle at the corners. She grabs a menu and beckons for me to follow her. We weave through the crowded tables for a couple of moments before she seats me near a beautiful stone water feature near the center rear of the restaurant.

The moment she leaves me with the menu and a glass of iced lemon water, I'm instantly regretful of the seating choice. I look around at the small round table, the freshwater lily centerpieces, the candles glowing softly in smoked glass votives. This feels way too intimate for a meeting with a coworker, especially one of the same sex. I don't want to feel uncomfortable and I don't want that for Nikki, either. Maybe I should set up at the bar and take the pressure off both of us.

Or maybe I'm the only one who feels it?

I start trying to flag the hostess down to have her move me just when Nikki sees me waving. Damn it; too late now.

And good lord, what is Nikki wearing?

I hardly recognize the woman floating through the throng toward my table. I had no idea it was Nikki that J and I were dealing with at the club until the very last moment, and even then, the dim lighting in those rooms – and literal masks on that night – didn't allow for a full visual experience. I've never seen this version of Nikki before. She is the picture of utter confidence, slinking toward me with a skin-tight leather wiggle dress with a plunging neckline and sky-high stilettos. She's slicked her dark hair into a low, tight chignon. It suddenly made me feel underdressed in my work suit, like I should have gone with my first mind and gone home to change.

"Hey there, Boss." Nikki grins at me as she approaches and its brilliance in this environment hits me like a bolt of lightning.

"Uh, hi! Oh…," I realize belatedly she's reaching out to hug me and I respond a second too late, causing our arms to bump awkwardly as she was already in the process of retreating. We both chuckle. At least this whole thing isn't as uncomfortable as it had been.

She sits down across from me and I realize I haven't stopped staring.

Nikki widens her eyes at me, but at least she's still smiling. "I got lipstick on my teeth?"

As if her red lip and smoky eyeshadow were anything less than perfect. "No," I say quickly, coming back to myself as I settle back into my own chair. "You just…wow, you look amazing. I feel underdressed."

Cocking her head at the compliment, Nikki says, "Thanks! And don't worry about that; you look great. I have somewhere to be later on tonight and didn't want to change there."

Her explanation makes total sense. What doesn't is the fact that I can't keep my eyes off her no matter what I do. I'm so disturbed by this, I don't know what to do with my hands. I fumble through my drink order when the waiter comes by.

Alright, I need to stop thinking and do what we came to do – talk. "So, how was your day?"

Nikki bursts out laughing in a high, tinkly giggle that reminds me of bells ringing. "I imagine about the same as yours, considering I was in the same room with you for the majority of it."

God, instant cringe. What am I, twelve years old?

I hide my burning face in my palms. "You're totally right. That was stupid."

"You're probably as burned out as I am after that meeting. Especially with the way you got into everybody's ass about the budget. Very impressive, by the way."

I blush. *Blush.* What the fuck is happening right now?

I pull hard on the reins to my conscious mind and pull it up short. I'm not going to entertain *anywhere* it's trying to take me with physical reactions like that.

It must do the trick because Nikki and I begin to fall back into some semblance of the former camaraderie we shared in the past with surprising ease. I find the tightness in my neck and shoulders relaxing once more. I find myself laughing hard and loud like I used to with her whenever we'd shoot the breeze during and after work.

I feel like we've just hit our conversational stride when the food arrives: some salmon and veggies for me; some fancy sea bass and truffle plate for her. My mouth waters the instant the decadent steam from my plate hits my nose. I am *starving.*

We dig into our meals in a silence more comfortable than I can remember, and I realize I am really glad I came.

Nikki clears her throat. "I still want to talk to you about that night."

My heart stops for what feels like a full two seconds and I stare at her. I *was* glad –

"Look, let me say my peace," Nikki says in a hurry, most likely reading the negativity of my expression. "I need to get this out. I have been for a long time now."

Licking my lips, I put down my fork, swallow my mouthful of food, then gesture for her to continue.

"If you want the absolute truth, I want to apologize to you, Brooklyn. I am so sorry if I ever made you feel uncomfortable at any point that night. Especially when it comes to J. It was just…" Nikki pauses, eyes searching the ceiling as she grabs at the right words to use. "It was emotional for me, the 'surprise' part of that night. But I promise you, I don't regret any of it."

I swear, it's just one shock after another today. I'm not sure how much more I can handle. I don't even know how I feel about it right now.

Relieved?

Excited?

I'm not sure, but I do know I'm feeling a little less afraid of my own truth in light of Nikki's revelation. "I have some truth for you, too, then."

Nikki's eyes widen a fraction. "Really?"

"I was more worried about you freaking out and feeling uncomfortable than I was for myself, overall. I, uh" – a chuckle escapes me – "actually had a really great time. W-with the three of us." My heart is beating so fast again it's becoming hard to breathe.

Nikki's eyes narrow at me in some unknown contemplation, the fingertips of one hand drifting over one of her bare collarbones as a bit of color appears in her cheeks. "Is that right?"

"It is."

"That's good to know." This time it's Nikki who breaks eye contact. She tries to hide her smile by forking another bite of her fish. "That was probably the best time I ever had there, if you wanted to know."

"Also good to know." I wet my lips and catch her gaze again with a smirk of my own, finding something unmistakably heated there that reminds me vividly of the night we're discussing. "And, just for my clarification, what exactly did you mean when you said you had dealings with J at the club in the past? In the interest of transparency." J had been so vague about it when I asked him; maybe she'll be more open with me, woman to woman.

"Like I told you," Nikki says, with no hesitation whatsoever. "We had a handful of playtimes and that's it. But nothing like with us three together." Then she tilts her head and throws a smile at me again, the same one that is making me question where the warmth beginning to flood my body is coming from – the glass of wine we ordered with dinner, or from Nikki herself. I can't tell anymore, and that's not a good thing when it comes to J and me.

"Can I ask you something?"

When I look up again, Nikki is giving me a look I can't interpret and I'm not sure I want to. I swallow hard, my throat suddenly bone-dry despite all the liquid I've consumed. "Sure."

"Do you think the party that you, J, and I had at the club is something you'd want to do again, on purpose this time?"

I'm glad I wasn't holding my wineglass right then because I certainly would have dropped it. My hand lay still on the table, as frozen as my mind as I try to come up with an answer for her and fail every time.

Do I want that? Would J, considering his warnings about Nikki?

I'm not sure how long I fall quiet, but before I can answer, Nikki's hand reaches out and covers mine on the table, baby soft and warm.

The heat that curls slowly in my lower abdomen right then lets me know for sure this feeling isn't merely due to the wine. Part of me wants this girl – friend or not, coworker or not, in a relationship with J or not. But I can't say that out loud.

I gasp when I feel the warmth of her other hand bloom on my knee, under the table. The smile she gives me then reminds me very much of the devilish emoji she sent me earlier.

Nikki is gently stroking my knee and the back of my hand, her interest made crystal clear, and though most of me wants to, I can't make myself pull away.

At first. The thunderbolt of guilt that hits me immediately after makes it much easier. I move my knee but hold on to Nikki's hand. I don't know why, but right now, I need this connection with her.

I need some time to think about this before I talk to J. He can stay in the dark for a little while.

Chapter

Seven

More than once in the days after my dinner with Nikki, I wonder if the guilt and worry that settled deep in my gut has taken up a permanent residence there, like some kind of morality tapeworm eating away at all my happy thoughts – thoughts I should be having about J. Robbing me of my appetite. Creating shadowy hollows beneath my eyes.

I didn't expect it to affect me this much. I didn't expect *any* of this.

Nikki, on the other hand, has the rock-solid constitution of a hardened criminal, I guess. She's taken to bringing me lunch again almost daily, like she did in days of old when life was far less complicated. And I didn't envision her stripping and feeding me one of her full breasts whenever we shared some pasta salad.

What happened to the days when all I could think about was J and me twisted into some kind of sexual pretzel, sweating and swearing?

I didn't know how Nikki did it.

Being constantly around J has made it beyond difficult to focus on the relationship we're supposed to be building together. The guilt is heavier in his presence. More uncomfortable, like a tight leather coat in the middle of August, weighing me down from the inside out.

Even now, with my knees tucked tightly against my chest as I nestle into the corner of the couch in J's living room, I stare straight ahead and can barely tell what's happening on the television.

I blink and try to refocus after having checked out mentally a half-hour ago. Oh yeah, some horror movie with idiotic characters constantly putting themselves in danger and making stupid decisions… I purse my lips, my neck warming a little. I might actually be describing myself.

God, even if this movie's inane plot is the height of its genre, whatever's happening in my mind and heart right now is far more terrifying for my future than whatever is taking place on the screen.

I suppress a sigh at J's movie choice. Under normal circumstances, I love campy horror movies, but I don't have it in me to enjoy one tonight.

I hazard a glance out of the corner of my eye and find him still sitting close by my side, quietly munching on handfuls of popcorn from the large, glass bowl on his lap.

J doesn't seem to notice me looking at him through my lashes, but I can sense the instant his body catches on by the way his long legs suddenly flex open wider and he sinks deeper into the couch.

My lips press together. It's subtle, but through the glass bowl and remnants of popcorn kernels, I can make out the unmistakable bulge growing larger at the apex of his gray sweatpants.

The fact that J is wearing sweatpants at all twists yet another little knot into my already tight stomach. There was a time when he wouldn't be caught dead in a pair of sweatpants in his home by himself, let alone on the street. Yet, he knows how much I gush whenever he throws on the pair I bought on a whim to tease him. He hasn't worn them in a while, but he is tonight. Most likely just for me.

I swallow hard, my throat immediately too dry and tight for comfort, and point my gaze back at the television so I can pretend to be interested. Some half-naked teen is running for her life through the woods, and honest to God, I can relate to the feeling right now. My heart is racing.

How in the world is the thought of having sex with J right now producing this level of anxiety?

If I'm being totally honest with myself, it's straight-up fear that's slicking my palms with sweat – fear that sex with him won't be the same or that J will see the doubts lurking in the depths of my eyes. Fear that after all this time and all these years in which I thought what I have with J was exactly what I wanted, it might not be after all.

I'm terrified of what that means, especially if I have to start the process of figuring out that part of my life all over again from scratch.

If J can sense my misgivings, he doesn't let on, not even when my entire body tenses the moment he finally puts the empty popcorn bowl aside on the coffee table littered with the remains of our dinner.

I'm so wound up I actually jump when his hands find my ankles to pull my legs straight and my bare feet into his lap.

I stare at him, chest heaving. "What are you doing?"

"You don't like foot massages anymore?" He cocks his head at me, biting at the fullness of his bottom lip – a move that would normally have me jumping on top of him in a heartbeat. Now, though, it stalls the movement of air in my lungs and makes me forget to blink.

The room quiets – aside from the screams of terrified campers in the movie – and he waits patiently for my answer, watching without a visible ounce of the tension I'm feeling.

Okay, I'm overreacting. The man is only trying to give me a foot rub, not relax me to prepare for some interrogation about the meaning of my aberrant behavior lately.

I force my shoulders to relax and my face to melt into an easy smile. "I still think foot massages are pretty great, actually. Especially if you're the masseuse." My fingers find my gold necklace and fiddle with the pendant, easing my tension a little more.

"In that case…" J's deep voice trails off as he gets to work, briskly rubbing his palms together to warm them before placing them gently on both of my feet at once.

My head tips back against the arm of the couch as a soft groan escapes me. It deepens when he starts to work his thumbs with firm and deep strokes up and down each of my arches. I've forgotten how good he is at this.

"You seem more stressed than usual, Gorgeous," J says without looking at me, and I almost release a dark chuckle without an ounce of humor. He doesn't know the half of it.

I nod and sigh instead. "A little. Work's been kind of…" I try to choose my words with the utmost care. "Hectic."

He grunts in response, so I let him concentrate and refocus on the movie again. Those ridiculous kids really don't hear the madman running up the road with a chainsaw? I shake my head and reach for my glass for a sip of the wine left over from dinner. Such a stupid movie. Nikki would be having a grand time throwing popcorn at the TV if she —

I manage to catch myself before I chuckle aloud. No. Absolutely not. I will *not* think of my assistant while my very yummy boyfriend rubs my feet, blissfully unaware of my mental treachery. I am not that horrible of a girlfriend. I'm not that horrible of a *person.*

Am I?

If not, why is a running roll of ideas to get out of having sex tonight running through my mind?

If a saner person than me asked what it is about Nikki that is so attractive to me, I couldn't even nail it down. She doesn't dress any differently than she always has in the years she's worked for me. Our conversations at work aren't dramatically more salacious than they were prior to the BDSM club debacle, and I've always enjoyed her sassy personality and respected her sense of loyalty.

Perhaps it's the combination of all the things I like about her and the fact that she and I also seem to have this intense physical chemistry outside of work that is making me so loopy. I don't think it was there before. Or maybe it was, and it took an orgy to open Pandora's box.

Now I don't know if there's a way for me to go back to being clear headed when it comes to her.

Shit, this is so bad —

I screech and almost fly off the couch when J's nails dig into the sides of my calves out of nowhere.

My head whips back around to face him. "J, what the hell – "

"You know, I'm going to have to punish you if you keep ignoring me all night."

The look of pure devilment in J's narrowed eyes makes my tart reply fizzle out in my mouth and my racing heart come to a screeching halt in my chest. Jesus Christ. I haven't seen that look in what feels like forever, definitely before we decided to give a real relationship a shot. I didn't realize until this moment how much I've missed it.

J looks like he could eat me alive and I really, really want him to try.

Movie forgotten, he grabs me by the waist and yanks me down closer to him on the couch, getting up on his knees so he can loom over me.

"Open," he says, his voice steely and low with the command as he presses a finger into my suddenly very eager mouth. With a moan, my eyes slip closed and I oblige him with a sense of abandon that surprises even myself. I take my time with his finger to remind him of what I'm capable of, swirling my tongue around the tip before teasing my way down each side, warm and wet. When I open my eyes again, J's pupils are so dilated they look black and I – for the briefest of seconds – am almost afraid of what he might do to me.

Almost.

We stare at each other with deep, heaving breaths. This part of us – the wild, feral element to our relationship – is what I realize I've been yearning for. This is the part that makes me feel most alive. It's been some time since J all but abandoned his teaching role in our sex life as I came more into my own in that department, and interludes like this between us have become few and far between. Especially since the two of us agreed to commit to a more traditional relationship.

I suppose I never thought I'd have to sacrifice this aspect of our life to do it.

But the part of him that nurtures that same part of me, the part that lives on the razor's edge of what is right and acceptable in this world, showed up tonight. That's why I don't want to waste a second of this drowning in my own thoughts and fears.

J removes his finger and immediately eases it between my legs, slipping into my damp panties and circling my swelling clit with a gentle stroke, a perfect mirror of what I was doing to him with my tongue. My back arches, the anticipation making my toes curl and my legs restless. I whine as a warm, rolling heat begins to build in the pit of my stomach.

J's answering groan sounds loud as he buries his face in my neck, breathing deeply before dropping wet kisses along the shell of my ear and down the column of my throat.

So romantic. So… shit, so *unsatisfying*.

I need more. My heart is pounding with my craving, my hands trembling when I help J wriggle out of his sweatpants and he snatches my panties down my legs.

He's kissing me. I feel the hot, wet softness of his tongue on my bare stomach now, moving lower past my belly button the way I assumed he would. His nails dig into the flesh on the underside of my thighs but not as sharply as they did before, the pleasure distant and somehow out of reach. Making me desperate.

An image flashes through my mind, quick as a blink: Nikki in her black dress at dinner, offering me a sensual smile with her hand creeping up my thigh.

A gasping moan rises in my throat. I can't help it, but at least in this context, I don't have to hide it from J.

God, I have to stop this. I shake my head as if I can physically dislodge the errant thoughts and refocus on the delicious man between my legs, feasting on my pussy like it is his last meal and a sumptuous one at that. I ignore the fact that I have to consciously buck my hips against his face instead of them doing so on their own when the pleasure becomes too much.

This, making love to my man on the couch in his apartment, is all I've ever wanted.

It is.

I swear.

J positions himself at my entrance and slides in all the way to the hilt with no preamble, ripping a surprised gasp from me, then he is fucking me hard, pushing my knees up near my ears.

Yes.

Yes.

He immediately falls into that cadence I love, a slow, deep thrust I can feel from the pit of my stomach to the small of my back. A keening cry starts to build in my chest. He's panting in time to his rhythm. My own exhalations puff out of my throat at the same time. The tingling begins at the base of my spine, curling upward, drawing heat to the surface of my skin already covered in a sheen of sweat.

My eyes go wide yet again when J's huge hand finds the column of my throat and squeezes, the pressure tap-dancing on being too much. It makes it hard to swallow, but it also makes my clit swell a little more.

J's other hand flies between us as if he could sense the change in my physiology in that moment and he begins stroking my tender nub of flesh with four fingers slick with his own saliva.

His hips keep pumping. His hand keeps stroking. A buzz starts up in my body and I can sense an orgasm on the horizon, but… it's still so far away.

Why is it not coming any closer?

My entire body tenses once again as a sense of panic starts to cloud my arousal. This has *never* happened. No matter what is going on with me or how stressed out I might be, it has never been this difficult to reach a climax with J, and I… I don't like what that could mean.

I don't want this to be the beginning of the end.

Closing my eyes, I try to get a grip. I can't believe it's come to this, but a girl has to do what she has to do. If I happen to let my mind wander a bit to get the job done – just this one time – no harm, no foul. It's not as if J would know, and I certainly would never tell him I had to tap into my spank bank to get across the finish line.

J roughly grabs my hip and tugs, distracting me. When I open my eyes, he tilts his head to indicate he wants me to flip over.

Even better.

I happily oblige and roll onto my knees, spreading them wide and bracing myself with my elbows on the arm of the couch to give him easy access. He doesn't wait a moment before plunging back into my depths, and no matter how many times we do this, that initial entry always takes my breath away. At least that hasn't changed between us.

He's inside me deeper with each stroke than he was before, and I'm legitimately finding it hard to fill my lungs with air each time. The pleasure starts to rebuild, making me whine with every jiggling bounce of my ass off his chiseled torso.

My eyes screw shut. Sweat beads on my upper lip.

Come on. *Come on.*

I'm so close.

"Ow!" My neck snaps back when J grabs my hair and yanks my head backward, giving the shell of my ear a long, wet swipe from his tongue.

"Stop pretending you don't want to come," he says in a breathless whisper. From the way the muscles in his thighs are tensed against mine, I can tell he's holding himself back for my sake.

God, I'm trying.

For a moment, I consider faking it just to get this over with, but the desperate thought alone is the equivalent of a bucket of ice water being dumped on my naked body. I shiver in revulsion at the very idea.

J thinks my body's reaction is because of him and starts pounding me harder.

Shit, I'm starting to go numb down below.

Desperate times and all that…

I release the flood of thoughts I've been trying to hold back all night – Nikki's smile, Nikki's dress, Nikki's hand on my thigh… my first time on my own in a real orgy at the BDSM club.

The tingles come back with a vengeance at that thought, so I chase it down in my mind like my life depends on it.

My naked body tied to an uncomfortable wooden chair in the center of the viewing room in full view of the crowd watching on the other side of the glass, the soft nylon ropes cutting off my circulation.

The hot red welts on the insides of my thighs from the caning I've endured.

The carnal sound of at least fifteen different men moaning at the sight of my dripping wetness as they stroke their cocks to the cadence of my panting.

The orgasm that rips through me the instant the first hot shot of cum splashes against my entrance, rolling on and on as they coat my entire pussy and inner thighs, a slick layer of their combined semen dribbling down my skin as a gorgeous, buxom redhead crawls over between my legs to lap it all up –

"Oh, *fuck!*"

There it is.

Rather than slip through my fingers this time, the memories tumbling through my head finally light the fuse to my sexual dynamite and I implode in a matter of seconds at the visual, just as J gives a final painful tug on my hair and roars into his own climax above me.

My lungs feel too small and I can barely catch my breath as I sag back onto the couch.

With the movie credits having rolled some time ago, the only sound in the room now is our combined ragged panting. I sit back and run my fingers through my mussed curls, cheeks flushing because I can feel J's eyes on my face.

Maybe he knows. Maybe he knows I wasn't thinking of him the moment I came.

Shaking my head, I'm off the couch and righting my dress before my brain fully registers the movement. Where's my coat?

"Where are you going?"

J's voice sends a pang of regret that peals inside my body like a bell, but I can't stop to look at him. I need some distance – some space. I need to think.

"I'm starving," I say, plucking my coat off the wall hook by the front door and stuffing my arms haphazardly into the sleeves. "There's a bodega down the street that sells this sandwich I love; they're the only ones that do around here. I'll be right back."

J is intelligent enough to know it's bullshit. As do I. But it's a necessary evil right now.

Without a backward glance, I close the door behind me and dash off into the night.

CHAPTER

Eight

I've never been so grateful to have a key to another person's apartment. I manage to barely make a sound when I creep back into J's place after having been gone almost – I check my watch – *three hours?* Shit, I didn't think I'd been away that long.

To be fair, I *did* go down to the bodega and grab a snack like I'd told J I planned to do, but afterward I munched on my *platanos* and wandered the street like I had nowhere to go. It was nearly as crowded after midnight as it is during the day in this part of the neighborhood. No one paid me any attention and it felt good to let my mind go blank, forcing out all thoughts like a sieve to simply enjoy the salty-sweet flavor of plantain in my mouth and watch the movement of my feet on the dirty pavement.

But I couldn't stay gone forever. I hoped J would be asleep by the time I got back.

I don't dare call his name when I turn the knob to his bedroom door and peek through the crack I make.

The lights are off, but I can make out the shape of him in the bed amongst the rumpled sheets and comforter, one dark arm thrown over his head.

I pause for a moment to listen and find J's breathing deep and even.

A miracle, but I won't dare look a cosmic gift horse in the mouth. Especially when I actively ignored every one of the texts he sent me while I was gone.

Each message was terse and unlike him. I realized I was testing his limits by not replying, but I just… couldn't. He's been trying so hard to give me what I want – what I *thought* I wanted. Hell, what I *think* I want? Maybe?

Probably?

I don't know. That's why I needed to think. Why I still do, even though with how horrible a girlfriend I'm being at the moment, I don't deserve J's infinite patience.

He doesn't move when I slip into bed beside him after stripping out of my clothes.

Bit by bit, I release my held breath and try to relax when it's clear he's not going to wake up and curse me out like I halfway expect him to.

At least another hour passes by and sleep still doesn't come. I can't do anything with these thoughts buzzing through my mind like stinging insects, so I lie there and stare into the darkness.

It doesn't have any answers for me, either.

Biting my lip, I pat around the nightstand as quietly as I can, feeling around for my cell and holding my breath with the hope I don't knock off anything heavy and wake up J.

I get the device into my hand without mishap, so I quickly turn the brightness on the screen all the way down and check my messages.

I got a "hey, girl" from Sherry, reminding me I need to call her up for dinner sooner rather than later. The nonsensical video she sent along with her message of some dude twerking in a diaper nearly makes me snort out loud with laughter, but I hold it in.

The smile her message leaves on my face vanishes when I pull up the text thread between my sister and me.

My last eleven – no, *twelve* – texts have gone unanswered.

I feel a frown settling heavily between my brows as I toggle through the screens to get to my call log and see half as many outbound calls to her number, also unanswered.

That sick, heavy feeling resettles in the pit of my stomach, and I hate how common it's starting to become.

I heave a silent sigh, my eyes stinging with the surprise threat of tears.

I don't know what happened. I could have sworn the other week everything in my life had finally fallen into place and I was *happy*. Then I wake up one morning and everything has gone to shit.

My troubles with J and Nikki aside, an unsettling sense of dread for my little sister is starting to settle deep into my bones like the bitter cold of a Nor'easter wind.

Tossing my phone to the side of the mattress in frustration, I stare back at the ceiling again. With everything going on, I doubt I'll be able to sleep at all.

Fatigue makes me a liar. I must have fallen asleep between one long blink and the last because dappled sunlight is suddenly filtering through the blinds. A wide yawn makes my jaw crack.

For half a second, I forget that J and I have some very unpleasant unfinished business just before last night comes rushing back – the anxiety, the shame, the confusion – twisting my chest into a tight knot that rivals the one already taking up residence in my stomach.

Might as well get this over with. Hopefully the general chill of the early morning – and the fact that it's J's favorite time of day – will take the sting out of what I need to say. At least, once I figure out what the hell *that* is. I'm gonna have to wing it.

I roll over… and find J missing, the pale cream sheets rumpled around the empty spot on his side of the bed. I reach out a hand to run it across the fabric and find it cool to the touch. Well, he didn't just get up.

When I pause to listen intently, I pick up faint clinking and shuffling sounds coming from the direction of the kitchen, so at least J's still in the apartment. I was worried that I'd wake up to a note from him telling me to get out and never come back.

Guilt makes me tidy up the bed once I crawl from beneath the sheets, my body impossibly heavy. I can't remember the last time I felt this drained.

I try to ignore the slight tremble of my hands as I rush through my morning routine, making use of the toothbrush and other toiletries J always keeps for me in the house.

Remorse washes over me in yet another noxious wave. Look at that… something as simple as a supply of pretty, pastel toothbrushes under the sink and a discreet marble box for the tampons I leave here show how hard J has tried to show me a real relationship is what he wants.

I duck my head to suck some water straight from the faucet to rinse my mouth of toothpaste suds before spitting into the sink with a little more violence than I intended. I just… I just don't know how I got to *this* point so quickly. I used to be so sure of what I wanted. It was *easy*.

Now, though? Now I blink and everything comes apart in front of my eyes, like too many loose threads pulled at one time, leaving the beautifully woven tapestry of my life in ruins.

There's no reason for me to still be in this bathroom, staring at my sallow reflection in the mirror. I know it. I know that J knows it, especially because he hasn't called out to me enticingly the way he normally would when I linger in the bedroom for too long before breakfast.

I flex my hands again and again, gnaw at my lip, stare up at the morning shadows gathering on the ceiling. Anything to buy some more time to work up my nerve to meet J in the kitchen.

What am I going to say to him, really? Tell him that Nikki propositioned me? That I'm finding myself more and more attracted to her? That I… that these days I feel more like myself raising hell at the BDSM club than I do hanging out with him at his place or mine?

Shaking my head, my tense, clawed hands curl into fists.

Time to face the music.

I felt much braver standing alone in the bathroom than I do when I pad barefoot across the gleaming marble floors to the kitchen, where J is waiting for me.

"Good morning." J looks up at me from the table, his loose workout shirt clinging to the hard curves of muscle carved into his arms. I don't see the usual warmth in his eyes.

The lack of it lodges a solid lump in my throat. I barely manage a murmured hello as I sit down across from him and reach for the stainless-steel French press full of coffee.

J doesn't speak again, but he does grab a full plate off the counter and slides it toward me on the table. Bacon, extra crispy – almost burnt and exactly the way I like it. Hard scrambled eggs with cheese. Toast that's barely brown with honey and butter.

I swallow hard. It would seem my man knows me and what I want a little better than I know myself.

The wave of guilt crests again and I start to feel physically ill.

"Thank you for breakfast. You didn't have to do this." I smile up at him after taking a few delicious bites, but I can feel my smile go brittle and I can't hold it in place for long.

He doesn't say "you're welcome" or smile in response, just gives me a short nod and keeps eating.

The silence in the room pounds against my eardrums. Why didn't he turn on the TV or radio? I can barely stand it.

My hunched shoulders begin to creep up around my ears. I can't relax. The muscles in my neck and back are so tight they start to ache and I squirm in my chair to try and relieve the pressure.

God, I should just tell him how I feel. About everything. Maybe it won't be so bad. Maybe… maybe by telling him out loud, I can also tell myself and everything can be clear again.

My eyes flip up to J's to find him staring at me with an expression I can't decipher, something like impassive disinterest tinged with hurt.

My eyes begin to burn in response.

Anything I tell him now will only hurt more. I can't do it.

That makes me a coward, but I'm not strong enough for that particular conversation today.

So instead, I say, "Is this bread from that new bakery down the street you took me to a couple of weeks ago – "

"What changed for you since we decided to try for a real relationship?"

J's sudden and very pointed question kills the silly one I was about to ask. Blinking at him in surprise, I'm not sure how to answer.

I slowly put down my fork with a clink that sounds louder than it should and take a long sip from my mug of black coffee. The heat that crawls up my neck and into my face has little to do with the consumption of my hot drink.

Folding my hands on the table, I force myself to look in his eyes when all I want to do is run away from this conversation. But it's necessary. "Um, I'm not really sure, to be honest with you. Nothing in particular *happened,* necessarily."

J's expression doesn't waver, and it's already driving me insane that I can't tell what he's thinking or feeling. "Do you not want to be in a relationship, then?"

My eyes close as the question runs through me like a blade in my chest. It's the same one that's been bouncing around in my head for weeks now, me running from it the entire time, but now I have no choice but to face it.

Do I want to be in a relationship?

If it were anyone but J, no, I don't think I would.

I open my mouth to answer, but J is onto another question before I have time to speak.

"I guess the better question would be: do you want to be in a relationship with *me?*"

It's like he can read my mind.

Taking a deep breath, I hold it for a second and then release it all in one long *whoosh.* "I don't know." My voice sounds weak and sad to my own ears as I try for a naked kind of honesty that makes me feel like hiding under the table. "I'm not completely sure what I want anymore. But I do know that I want *you.*"

Finally, I catch a flicker in J's gaze as he studies me, something like recognition, and perhaps hope.

It bolsters me with enough courage to pose my own query, one that has been gnawing at me for a while now. "What's changed for *you?*"

A frown creases his forehead. "For me? What do you mean?"

I shrug. "Your whole… the vibe has been different for a minute."

"My 'vibe.'" He purses his lips in thought. "I still don't know what –"

"We haven't been back to the club in months, J."

The words are out of my mouth before I realize I've spoken; my obsessive attention to the issue in my mind has given them a life of their own. I didn't intend to sound so angry, but I suppose that's how I feel. It's like J took something I loved away from me without realizing it. An entire aspect of our relationship disappeared overnight.

When I stop to examine it, I've been feeling like I'm being punished for some infraction I wasn't aware of and I am starting to resent J for it.

Hurt returns to J's eyes in response, but I don't back down, resisting the compulsion to do so. I don't want to hurt him by any means, but we need to let the light of truth back into this gray space between us.

After a long, heavy pause, J speaks again. "Why are you acting like I forbade you to go?"

"Oh, I know you didn't *forbid* me, but –"

"We can go back whenever you want. It's not a problem."

"I – really?" My jaw slackens in surprise. "You'd still want to come with me?"

"Of course." He sips at his coffee, the first smile I've witnessed all morning, flirting with his full, luscious lips.

I sit back in the chair, sporting my own answering grin. "Okay," I say, and nibble on my honeyed brioche.

Never mind that I still haven't said a word about Nikki, or that I know practically squat about J's family or his life before we met after all this time together. Those are all battles we'll have to fight another day. The point is that he and I survived this one intact and, above all, *we are going back to the BDSM club.*

The joy that bursts through my body like sparklers beneath my skin is embarrassing, I'll admit. I'll also learn to live around the guilt that has apparently taken up a permanent residence in my heart.

I am going to be me again. J and I are going to be *us*. That's all that matters.

CHAPTER

Nine

One thing I can say I love about J is that he is absolutely a man of his word.

We arrive in high style at the very next BDSM-themed party a week or so after our heavy conversation regarding the state of our relationship.

It's "White Night." Everywhere we look, fashionable attendees strut around in finery in every shade of the color, from ecru to eggshell to diamond white, dressed to the nines. It's especially crowded tonight, with far more people than I can remember being here the last few times I attended by myself. As I peer through the crush of bodies, I even catch a glimpse of a crystal-studded ball gown or two. These people did not come to play.

The excitement bubbling in my veins rivals the effervescence of the glass of champagne in my hand, my second already. We've only arrived twenty minutes ago at the most.

Standing next to me, so close I can feel the heat of his body through his clothes, J leans down and I think he's going to whisper something in my ear. Instead, he lets his lips brush my earlobe. I can't help but shiver despite the warmth in the room from all the people milling around us.

I smile up at him, pleased to no end that I don't have to force it anymore, and the smirk he offers in return appears to be just as genuine.

He's such a good sport. J went so far as to don an all-white outfit to coordinate with mine like we're at a school dance instead of a sex fest with the potential to get very messy; his loose, ivory turtleneck and slacks match my sweater dress that bares the curve of one shoulder and the wide belt cinching my waist is the same camel color as J's leather loafers. We look like a perfect matching set. I'm relieved he doesn't appear to be too embarrassed about it.

After breakfast at his place the morning of "The Conversation," I worried my revelation about my desire to return to the club would make J feel insecure. He told me he's changed a lot about how he moves in relationships just for me – though Lord knows I still don't completely understand his modus operandi on that front – and I want to make sure he feels how much I appreciate his willingness. My chest aches with it.

I plan on riding with my better angels tonight instead of my baser nature. It's already calling me into the sexual fray, beckoning me to leave J's side and throw myself vagina-first into the revelry with my fellow hedonists. There will be time for all that, but not tonight.

Hundreds of people are among us at this moment, but J has decided to place his trust in the belief that I'm here only for him and our relationship and I plan on proving him right.

We move steadily toward the large stairs that lead to the playrooms hidden away below. The bubbly makes it easier to open my senses to take in all I can – the faint and inexplicable scents of buttered popcorn and spice, likely to hide the aromas of sex soon to permeate the air. The plushness of the fancy carpet beneath my white patent leather stilettos. The throb of sensuality underlying the words and laughter of all the attendees filling the space with sound. The warm sense of security that pulses through my body when J laces his long fingers through mine and holds my hand tighter.

J isn't holding back affection the way he was before, but I still can't shake off the stiffness lingering in my shoulders. Any false move I make tonight might send him back into his shell. I don't want to risk undoing the progress we've made.

The closer we come to the ground floor as we descend the wide staircase adorned with white silk swags and twinkling fairy lights, the more naked the people around us become. Spotting bare flesh amongst the fine fabrics in motion all around us becomes more and more frequent, until we find ourselves back in our old haunt – the massive playroom taking up the entire basement floor of the mansion with glass-walled viewing rooms on either side of the wide hallway.

It's like a Roman bacchanal down here. I don't know what it is about this particular themed night, but the electricity in the air produces goosebumps up and down my arms as I cling to J's elbow and watch couple after threesome after group grope and fondle and fuck each other right there in the hallway, designated rooms be damned. Did they pump pheromones in through the ventilation system or something? There's so much grunting and sighing going on it feels like we stumbled onto the set of an extremely explicit porno shoot.

A grin tugs at my mouth, begging to be set free. Can't say I mind too much. I love the way my heart thrums as I watch the sweaty spectacle unfold before us.

Out of nowhere, J presses me against one of the walls papered in some fancy silver fabric and grunts, pressing his hips into mine and making me gasp for more reasons than one.

"You up to playing tonight or just watching?" His voice sounds barely controlled in my ear and I close my eyes to savor it for a heady moment. The version of J I've been missing so much has arrived and I'm *so* glad he's here, at least for now.

When I look up into his eyes, however, the brown depths shine with a vulnerability I haven't seen there before.

There's a right and wrong answer to his question.

I gulp. My aching pussy already knows what it wants to do.

But my head and heart also know that's not why we're here. I have to keep my focus. My future is all tied up in this. In J. In *us*.

"We can watch," I say, as carefully as I can, squeezing his hands for emphasis.

This time J's smile reaches his eyes and they crinkle in the corners, the way they always used to whenever he looked at me. Before things changed between us so much.

He presses the softest kiss to the corner of my mouth. "Let's go."

I'm grateful I had the forethought to dust on my kiss-proof lipstick tonight, not knowing what kind of trouble I'd be getting into mouth-wise.

J starts to pull me toward our old faithful, one of the plush velvet loveseats placed before each of the viewing rooms. Now I know for sure I've never seen it this crammed with people before. Each one of the rooms is occupied with no less than four enthusiastic participants, a totally different expression of sexuality playing out in each space.

It's like a sexual buffet, and God, I am starving.

No, no. I will not blindly indulge my hunger pangs. To that end, I tug on J's hand. He turns back to me, brows raised in surprise as I lead him toward the far end of the long room instead. Toward the large, raised dais now occupied with a single, high-backed wooden chair, about the only piece of furniture in this place not currently in carnal use.

"Come on." We've never done this, and I'm taking a risk at embarrassing myself if I'm wrong in thinking he'll be okay with it. Jaw tight, I pull J up onto the platform carpeted with what looks like red velvet – a favorite fabric in this establishment – and maneuver him in front of me.

He stares down at my face, ignoring the crowd already coalescing behind me as I face him, their lustful gazes burning into my back. "I thought you said you only wanted to watch." He takes a fingertip and tucks one of my loose curls behind my ear.

The gesture makes heat flood my face and ears. Gotta keep it together. Reaching up, I run the pad of my thumb over one of his chiseled cheekbones. "I want to take care of you."

His eyes flash dangerously. I take that as my cue to press against his shoulders with both my hands. Slowly, he lets me push him down into the chair. Those same eyes alight with a sensuous fire as they watch me sink to my knees before him, kneeling like an eager supplicant before her king.

He'll feel like one tonight if I have anything to do with it.

Despite the moans and soft curses of appreciation I hear when I shrug out of my tight sleeves to let the top of my dress pool around my waist, I continue to let J's gaze consume me, making me feel more vibrant than I have in months. He doesn't look away when I unhook my bra and toss it onto his lap, letting my breasts tumble free with a solid bounce. My hands stroke the growing bulge between his thighs and he subtly writhes against the hard wooden seat of the chair.

J's chest starts to heave with now-audible breaths as I tease him, rubbing my breasts against his trousers, then my face, raking my clawed hands up and down the fronts and insides of his thighs until his hips start to buck toward me on their own.

The sounds behind me grow in urgency, stoking my own fires. I purposefully left my fancy panties at home and went commando, so I can feel the instant my wetness starts to increase in volume and drip down the insides of my legs.

I wish J could see it.

Then I remember where I am, that my desire to bare myself to him in every way in front of strangers is absolutely accepted and encouraged here, and immediately stand up long enough to shove my dress down over my hips and kick the whole thing to the side.

J's hands find the deep curve of my waist and slide down over the plump roundness of my bare ass.

I groan in amorous surprise when he yanks my cheeks apart with an aggressive sting of my tender flesh, baring all my hidden parts to the people behind me still watching us.

My skin feels like I've been doused in flames. If I'd still been in that sweater dress by now, I'd be dying.

Settling into a squat, I spread my knees when I do so to give J the best view of my swollen, glistening lips and our audience a look at the intricacies of my ass. I go in, pulling at J's pants, the mounting desire too intense for me to manage sedately.

J is thick and beyond hard when I release him from his prison of cotton and elastic, ready to do anything I want.

And I want to taste it, so I do.

I fist J's considerable girth, testing its weight in both my hands, planting soft, experimental kisses along both sides of his length until I hear him start to groan in time with my ministrations.

A devilish pleasure bursts in and floods my entire being. I glance up to find him staring at me with the sort of awe that nearly makes me come from the sight of it.

It's never been quite like this. I've always known J to be stern in the bedroom. Always teaching, always disciplining me. Never under my full control and at my mercy.

I have to say… it's intoxicating.

I want more of it.

My tongue takes it to another level. I explore him from root to tip, trying to memorize the mildly salty taste and silky-smooth feel of him with my mouth alone, as if it would have to last me a lifetime. I work at him, throwing my back into it, taking him deeper into my throat than I ever have, gagging and then gathering all the moisture into my hands to work up and down his shaft with firm fingers.

I'm still almost delicate about it. I don't want him to come. Not yet.

I want J to feel how much I still want him, that even though I don't know exactly how I want our relationship to look moving forward, I don't want to be in one with anyone else – not a man, at least.

The thought dampens my fire a bit, but the way J's knees begin to tremble brings me back to the moment. His hands clamping down on my shoulders anchor me to Earth. He hears what I've been trying to tell him with my hands and lips and tongue, and my eyes nearly tear up with relief because words have been failing me for so long this has become a last resort.

I suck and gag and suck some more, the crescendo of moans and sighs at my back egging me on. Jaw slack, J literally yelps when I take one wet hand and gently twist it around and around his bulging sac, now tightening in my palm with his impending orgasm.

My hand drops and I center myself within his gaze. As much as I love the feeling of J shooting his release all over my body, I want to feel the intensity of what we're doing in a different way than we've done it before.

J seems to read my mind. He hauls me up by my shoulders and captures my mouth in a ferocious kiss that I feel down to my toes. When he pulls back, he stares into my eyes with a tight grip on the base of his cock, and I know what he wants – the same thing I do right now.

Teetering precariously on my narrow high heels, I plant my feet on the stage on either side of his thighs and let my entire body drop hard into his lap.

A scream rips from my throat when I impale myself on him while J groans low and desperate, rubbing his face against my sweaty collarbone. He wastes no time bucking his hips beneath me, each thrust akin to lighting one stick of dynamite after another deep inside me.

It's not long before I'm ready to blow. My legs are shaking so hard I can barely keep myself upright. J grabs my hips, likely leaving purple thumbprints in my flesh as he spreads me wide and slams my ass down onto him again and again.

We're both panting and watching each other's faces, waiting for the telltale clouded eyes to signal our descent into mutual madness. I have no idea how many people are watching us by this point, but J and I might as well be the only people in the room. This feels more intimate than it ever has. If I look hard enough, I might be able to see his soul. Surely, he can see mine now, plain as day.

Even though this is the most tender we've ever been with each other in such a scenario, our natural inclinations begin to seep through our actions. He starts to go a little too deep. J's hands leave my hips to claw at my back. It all hurts so good I can't help but reach a hand out to his thick neck and *squeeze.*

I'm going to come so hard; J is already twitching inside me and I can tell he's just as close.

Hold on, baby. Just wait for me.

I want us to let go together, but frustration makes my hands tingle when movement in my peripheral area distracts me.

Something tells me to stay focused, but I can't fight the compulsion to look over my shoulder.

The moment I do, I look right at Nikki standing at the very front of the crowd, her dark eyes shimmering with lust.

CHAPTER

Ten

For a moment, I worry my soul may have left my body because I know for sure I've stopped breathing altogether.

Whether it's from shock or desire or absolute terror is anyone's guess, including mine. I suppose it may be a healthy serving of all three.

Nikki never said a fucking word about coming tonight, of all nights. We'd reached a semi-comfortable equilibrium after our dinner "date," reestablishing a sense of normalcy between us, at least at work. She knows I go to this club. She knows that I know *she* goes to this club. So, she had to know this was the biggest event of the year.

Did she plan it like this? To pop up on me when I least suspected it?

Jesus, how long has she been watching us anyway?

Doesn't matter because now I'm watching *her*. Nikki has adorned herself in sparkling white, wearing a gown with a hem that reaches the floor and has slits up either side that reveal the ample curves of her hips.

The finery she's sporting from the waist down is in comical contrast with the raciness of her top – a halter in the same fabric that bares her shoulders and has cutouts for her breasts shaped like hearts.

She's standing too far away for me to reach out and touch her if I wanted – and in this instant, I really, really do – but Nikki is still close enough to the dais for me to witness the exact moment her nipples harden as she watches my face.

That's about the time I feel J turn his head to look over my shoulder, to see what I'm staring at so hard. His intake of breath is silent but I feel his chest rise against mine all the same. Tension takes hold of his firm pectorals beneath my hands, and it's no longer because he's on the verge of a climax.

I don't look at him. I can't, not until I get a handle on the conflicting emotions coursing through my body in high tide, steadily washing my amorous feelings away to sea.

Nikki recognizes what she wants. I can see that in her kohl-lined eyes plain as day. The hunger. The need. But as her gaze holds mine, she hesitates.

I don't blame her. Everything I feel right now is reflecting right back at me.

There's no way to tell how long I'm frozen in this state, J still hot and hard deep inside me, my thighs trembling on either side of his on the wooden chair, my neck craning over my shoulder.

The truth begins to bubble up from the depths I've buried it for the night, forcing its way to the surface no matter how I finally clench my eyes closed and try to resist it. But it's there, and I know in my heart I want J. *And* I want Nikki.

Together. At the same time.

My inner muscles flutter around J's girth at the very thought and I feel his groan rumble against my neck, spurring me to action. I need to make a decision.

With everything that's happened tonight, J and I have taken a gigantic leap forward in our relationship, and I don't want to do anything to jeopardize that progress. But my sudden and debilitating need to feel Nikki's skin against mine – so soft and the color of butterscotch – is just as strong.

Nikki makes up my mind for me. She stalks onto the stage with the grace of a feline on the hunt, never tearing her eyes from mine.

Meanwhile, I catch the restless shifting of the crowd watching us in my peripheral vision as they wait with bated breath to see what we have in store.

Personally, I have no idea. Nikki comes to stand right next to J and me and all the remaining coherent thoughts in my head evaporate with the first olfactory hit of spiced vanilla from her perfume. A little smile twists one corner of her mouth, painted red as fresh blood. When she reaches out a bold hand to caress my bare shoulder, a shocked gasp fills my throat.

This feels so different than the last time we were here together, when I worshiped this skin and that mouth, blissfully unaware the owner of those lovely features was someone with whom I was already well-acquainted. Intention changes everything, charges the air, sends goosebumps racing across overheated skin.

Nikki wants me, I want her, and we both want J.

He seems to come to the same realization when Nikki and I turn to look at him in unison.

Strong fingers grip the flesh of my hips tighter. At the same time, I feel J swelling anew inside me. The bolt of pleasure it spears through my system makes my head tip back on a throaty moan.

Nikki and I aren't the only ones interested.

I look back to J again to find a troubled expression on his face – brows low, mouth pinched in the corners. Still, he can do nothing about the way his eyes glitter with unspent lust.

Placing a gentle hand on his cheek, I find myself begging with my eyes alone. I have been fighting this for so long and now relief from this need is right here in my hands.

Please.

If J and I had not spent enough time together over the past few months to get our nonverbal communication down pat, I would have missed his eventual agreement, but I catch his nearly imperceptible nod.

Yes.

Leaning forward to press my naked breasts against the heat of his chest, I throw myself into the kiss I land on his lips. J's grunt of surprise dissolves into a moan and his hips begin to rock very slowly against mine once more, leaving me breathless.

It's nearly painful to do so, but I pull away so I can reach a hand out to Nikki. She slips hers into mine after another pause, letting me pull her gently forward. After a tiny stumble, Nikki falls against J, catching herself with her palms flat on his chest and shoulder before she presses the softest kiss against the corner of his mouth. Giving him the chance and space to turn away if he so chooses.

He doesn't. Instead, J captures her mouth in a kiss passionate enough for me to feel it in the thrust of his hips. His tongue is in her mouth, her hands fist his curls. Desire hits me like a wrecking ball made of hot lead and I find I can't be jealous of their display if I tried – I'm too far gone already. I lean back, bracing myself on J's knees and spreading myself wide. J is practically in my chest, he's in so deep. With a grunt, I grind myself against him, sweat already dripping down the curve of my back.

Nikki breaks her endless kiss with J at last. Growing hotter under her stare, I work my hips against J even harder. The nakedness I feel as we look at each other has little to do with the amount of flesh I've exposed to her and everyone else in the room. But if Nikki isn't looking away to safety, neither am I.

She's on the prowl again, getting down on her knees so her face is level with the place where J and I are joined. That smirk doesn't leave her face when she bends down to swipe the flat of her tongue over my swollen clit and lower, sucking lightly at the base of J's cock with every upward surge he gives me.

I screech. Between that tongue and J's powerful strokes, it's too much. So soft and wet and warm I feel electric all over. A few more seconds of this and I'll come for sure, and I'm not ready for this to be over so soon.

It takes some doing to make sure I don't break an ankle, but I swing my leg over and maneuver myself off J's lap, falling into a squat on the opposite side of his thigh from Nikki. Eyes flicking back and forth between us, J grips himself with a firm hand and licks his lips.

He already knows where this is going. And so does Nikki, apparently; she dives tongue-first for his balls while I seize the whole of his manhood with my mouth alone.

My focus is on J above all. Or rather, I'm trying to keep it that way. Being so cool and open about Nikki joining us to play despite their questionable history – and J's ambivalent feelings toward her – feels like some kind of privilege after the way I've treated J lately and I don't want to abuse his trust in me. He didn't have to agree to come with me here tonight, but he did.

That doesn't ease the acute awareness of Nikki in my mind whatsoever, no matter how much I try to focus solely for the moment on J's pleasure. When I close my eyes, her scent fills my nose. The heat from her skin where we touch threatens to burn me to ash. Somehow, the two of us manage to gravitate toward each other still, until Nikki shifts her attention from the southern border of J's cock to the thick shaft itself. I'm already working up and down the sides with open lips and she does the same, until our mouths are sliding past that of the other with his girth sandwiched in between.

There's no way that's not intentional. On Nikki's part or mine. After a while, our movements become a sort of glancing kiss and shivers dance up and down my spine with the surprising intensity of it.

I… I can't let myself get lost in the feeling of her fulfilling my every fantasy – especially when her hands find my tits and squeeze, making me bite back a whimper. I hazard a glance up at J. He's watching us so intently I can almost feel it like a stroke down my back, his brow furrowed in concentration. His thighs tense when I swipe a bead of pre-cum away with the tip of my tongue.

"Nikki."

Hearing her name on J's lips out of nowhere makes me pause in surprise. By the time I realize what's happening, J has already reached for Nikki and settled her slim body down hard on his cock – and my head.

Her hips buck and she's already riding him and squealing as I duck to get safely out of the way and avoid breaking my neck.

Watching them triggers a painful twinge in my chest. J fucks her like he's done so for years; Nikki arches her back and rides his thrusts as if she belongs to him and her body has always known it.

Maybe this was a bad idea –

My brain doesn't have time to finish the negative thought and completely kill my libido. Nikki reaches behind her to grab my hand, placing it squarely on her ass.

It's as clear an invitation as I have ever received.

Nikki's moans have turned to guttural wails and I understand exactly what she's feeling from the way J's hands grip her hips and the chair starts to scrape against the ground with the power of his movements. I know too well how deep he can go, how much space he can take up in her body, filling her with an ecstasy she can hardly contain.

Something wild surges up in me and I have to taste them. Crawling forward on my hands and knees, I rear back and shove my face into the open space between J's open thighs to pay tribute to his balls with my tongue as Nikki had.

But it's not enough. I can't taste *her.*

Straining my neck, I reach up even higher, wordlessly seeking with my mouth until – God, right there. They're both moving, so I have to stick my tongue out pretty far to reach, but flicking it along the perimeter of Nikki's tight pussy as J slows to press his wide cock in and out of her earns me a fresh onslaught of moans from them both.

The heat in my blood is becoming unbearable. Carnal whimpers and shouts from the crowd echo my own. The tension coiling deep inside my core feels primed to snap.

Before I can slip a hand between my own thighs, however, J makes yet another move. Every muscle in his powerful legs makes itself known as he slides down off the chair to the floor so he's sitting with his back to the seat. One of his strong hands finds my forearm, hauling me upward.

Instinct lets me know what J has on his mind and I position myself backward on the chair, my ass hanging off the edge.

J never stops fucking Nikki, whose face and neck are dripping with sweat I'm tempted to taste. As soon as I've grabbed a hold of the chair back for balance, J's arms hook under my hips and he attacks my pussy with his hot mouth like it owes him money. I'm already so wet I'm about to sob my release in a matter of moments; my legs are back to trembling again.

My body feels like it's going to come apart when something soft and warm glides up my inner thighs, then over the mounds of my naked ass cheeks. Nikki's hands, reverent despite the hardcore fucking the three of us are doing. I can't see her face with my back to her, but the delicate nature of her touch tells me she's longed for this as much as I have.

I want to look at her, though. To see if I'm right. But I don't dare, even knowing J won't be able to see me do it with his face buried between my thighs. There may be a hot need waiting for me in Nikki's eyes, but who knows what else I might see? I could witness something dangerously tempting that'll make me fall into them and never return to my relationship, and I don't want to risk that.

So, I throw my head back and wiggle my hips over J's face, reveling in the feel of his soft tongue probing my depths.

Nikki won't be ignored. My eyes nearly pop out of my head and I scream the instant she adds her tongue to the mix, gliding wetly up and down the seam of my backside until finally circling my puckered opening with the very tip of her tongue, over and over as my flesh absorbs the vibrations of her moans.

Between the evident skill of her mouth and J's, I think I will come right out of my skin. It takes a second to realize the distant roar I hear is coming from my own throat. A release the likes of which I have never known is barreling toward me, and it will snap me in half when it arrives in all its glory.

Oh, my god…

So good…

So…

Oh –

Wait, what is that ringing?

My eyes snap open, my ears instantly picking up on a sound out of place amidst the groaning and yelps of pleasure filling the air all around us.

A siren?

Whipping my head around, I glance around the room at the bodies writhing below us in various states of undress. Everyone carries on with their business, as if I'm the only person who heard it.

I'd left my phone in the hidden inner pocket of my dress… is it my phone ringing?

As the high-pitched siren continues, unease creeps up my back and instantly cools the sweat on my skin. I need… I don't know why exactly, but I need to check my phone.

I pat J's arm with an impatient hand and ignore their dazed expressions when he and Nikki make way for me to move my stiff limbs off the chair and wobble over to the edge of the dais where I'd haphazardly tossed my dress aside. Ignoring the curious and confused stares being thrown my way, I squat down and fish around the soft fabric until I feel something hard.

I tug my phone free and stare at the screen with blood thrumming in my head.

Three missed calls from Bianca. So that had been my little sister's designated ringtone I'd heard.

Oh, no.

My heart stops when I see the text she sent immediately after she called: *911*.

CHAPTER

Eleven

My hands start shaking so hard I drop my phone.

I haven't had a proper conversation with my sister in weeks, and it wasn't from a lack of trying. I've lost count of how many of my calls and text messages have gone unanswered since the family dinner when I had tried to get her to tell me what was going on with her. Bianca showed up for family dinner every week, but she seemed… hollow somehow, the light gone from her normally happy expression and her eyes rimmed with dark circles.

Once she ate, she gave my mom, brother and me each a one-armed hug and fled into the night. And that was it.

Bianca would climb up a lightning pole in an electrical storm before she'd ask anyone for help. She's always been that way. When she was small, I was the one who usually found her dangling precariously off the top edge of the fridge in a quest for the cookie jar that had ended in misadventure. She'd giggle and clutch me with her sticky fingers before dashing off to enjoy her treat. Asking me to get the cookie for her was out of the question, even then.

Fear, cold and sharp, grips my insides and steals my breath. What in God's name could have happened for my sister to send an emergency text like this?

What if she's cold and hurt somewhere we can't get to her?

Or kidnapped?

Or –

No. My head drops into my hands as the phantom horror of the unthinkable washes over me in a sickening wave.

"Brooklyn!"

J's voice over my shoulder snatches my mind back to the here and now. I know what I have to do.

I need to get out of here.

My brain prompts my frozen limbs to animate as it shifts into auto-pilot – struggling into my sweater dress and trying to steady myself on my heels – all the while tumbling through every worst-case scenario my subconscious can dredge up for me to fixate upon.

When I stand and turn, I find J has extracted himself from Nikki's vagina and they both stare at me with wide, wondering eyes.

"Are you okay?" Nikki's impressive nakedness is as on display as J's, but the two of them stand near me as if their lack of attire in the face of my obvious distress is the most normal thing in the world. Her hand reaches for me but I spin away, already heading toward the exit.

"My sister," I say, and the words come out so guttural and broken they don't sound like they came from my mouth at all. "My sister is…" I can't finish. Saying anything aloud could make it true. "She needs me – I have to go. I'm sorry."

And I am, truly and deeply, because the three of us had been sharing something intense and uniquely beautiful that was primed to turn me inside out. I must have flown too high; the crash back to reality was too far a fall for it to leave me unscathed.

I run full out, kicking off my heels in order to pound up the main staircase absent of the fear of breaking an ankle, then dashing through the remains of the earlier crowd in bare feet to the dark of the street in front of the massive building.

God, what time is it, anyway? I'm straining to make out the digital clock on my phone's screen, but it's difficult because everything is suddenly so blurry… blinking, I squint against the burn behind my eyeballs and swipe at them with the back of my hand. When wetness gathers on my skin, I realize it's because I've been crying.

No time for any of that. Shaking my head, I begin to pace the sidewalk, ignoring the layers of filth and grime beneath my soles. My hands shake as I thumb through the screens of my rideshare app. How far would it be to –

Shit. I still don't know where Bianca is right now.

I pull up my phone log, tapping her name and number to make the call.

It rings and rings and then goes to voicemail.

So, I try again.

And again.

Each time, the fear and worry tie me up tighter. My breathing gets heavier and shallower and I feel myself teetering on the edge of sanity. I'm going to lose it if I don't hear from her soon.

My heels pound the concrete as I shift my weight again and again. The pain makes me wince with every step, but I can't stop moving. It's as if my brain won't work unless I'm in constant motion.

It's the guilt that finally knocks the wind out of me like a brick to the chest. My dear, sweet baby sister needed me. Had actually reached out after radio silence for weeks. And what was I doing at the time?

My eyes close of their own accord as my face burns despite the coolness in the night air.

Her supposedly responsible, level headed older sister was in the middle of a public threesome with her boyfriend and her assistant at work, their tongues licking my pussy and my asshole, respectively.

If I wasn't some sexual deviant, Bianca would have reached me since I nearly always have my cell nearby if not on my person, even at home. I could have stayed and hung out with J like he wanted. If I had, I would have heard my phone ring and been able to come to her rescue in whatever way she needs.

Then again… J and Nikki are hardly bad people, and Lord knows we all were enjoying ourselves. In recent hindsight, they both did what they could to ensure I didn't feel excluded – something I have to say I didn't expect – and I loved every second of our hands and lips and tongues on each other.

I could have given them a real explanation, if my mouth would have cooperated long enough for me to sound coherent.

Jesus Christ. I don't know what I'm feeling. Too many emotions coalescing into a noxious ball in the middle of my chest and I worry I'm about to pop.

What kind of sister am I?

What kind of *person?*

The crunch of leaves and plastic trash draws my watery eyes from the ground. Finally, a cab.

Yanking the door open, I slide into the back against the gray leather seats.

"Hey, hon." Blue eyes find mine in the rear-view mirror, but the darkness is too thick for me to make out any more of the driver's features. He may as well be some shadowy emissary from the gates of hell sent to bring me where I belong. "Where ya headed?"

I don't know. I don't know and that fact alone makes me want to throw my body up against the doors of this cab again and again in frustration.

Bianca could literally be anywhere.

"Hey, are you drunk? You need to get home? Where we goin'?"

"Uh, I'm sorry…" I grab my phone again and start up the futile scrolling through messages again. "I'm just trying to get a location for you…"

Location. That's it.

Hope swells inside of me. I forgot Bianca had shared her location with me a while back… I don't remember getting a notification that she'd stopped, so maybe I can use that to see –

Oh, thank God.

"Sorry, could you take me to this address?" I hold up my phone so the driver can see when he peeks at it over his shoulder. The blue glow illuminates his face for a second before he turns and his face disappears into the night's shadows again.

"Sure thing – not far from here."

Please, God.

Please let her be alright.

I force myself not to think about how long it's been since I set foot in church, or closed my eyes to pray for guidance instead of orgasms, or thought about someone other than myself and what I need.

And I'm not going to call my mother or my brother unless I absolutely have to. No sense in getting them all riled up and upset if I… if I find Bianca safe and in one piece.

My foot jiggles as I strain to see through the darkness in the part of the neighborhood we've entered, my gaze clinging to the glow of inter-mittent amber streetlights to reveal to me what lives and moves along the sidewalks.

The cab's brakes squeal as we come to a stop at the curb a few minutes later, just as the driver said. I look up at the sign just below the streetlight. A bus stop?

My body tears out of the cab before my brain can catch up, the fear I felt earlier returning ten-fold. There's someone on the bus stop bench, a female, with the hood of her coat thrown over her face.

I can't see if it's Bianca. I can't see the person's face and I slow as I approach. The last thing I want to do is potentially startle a stranger in the middle of the night and end up with my throat cut on top of everything else.

"Bianca." Even if the word hadn't come out as a dry croak, the stiff breeze rips it right from my lips. The person on the bench doesn't stir, so I don't think they heard.

My hands clench into fists. I lean over the sleeping form, reaching down to peel back the coat hood with the tips of my fingers so I don't wake them.

The motion makes the hood fall away, revealing my little sister's slack face and tears of relief practically burst from my eyes.

"Bianca! Bianca… baby girl, wake up." Fingers trembling, I run them over her, checking for signs of injury or damage. I feel lightheaded when I see nothing amiss or out of place. She's okay.

I… I'm so grateful she's okay.

Bianca's eyelids flutter, but I can tell she's out of it. The little bit of her eyes I can see looks glassy.

My baby sister is drunk off her ass. What the hell is she doing out here? Who left her like this?

The rage sweeps in just as quickly as the fear dissipates. I'm going to kill whoever abandoned her out here on her own. What if it hadn't been me who found her?

I'm going to make myself crazy with what-ifs and maybes, so I try to wake her up again. This time, Bianca groans but lets me guide her to her feet. She leans heavily into my side and I usher her into the cab and climb in beside her.

Once I give the cab driver the address to my apartment, we move away from the curb and hit the streets again.

It's impossible to tear my eyes away from Bianca, whose lolling head bounces against my shoulder every so often when we hit a pothole in the road. Questions crowd my mouth but I can't speak now if I wanted to. I cycle through emotions so quickly my body can't react to them appropriately – anger, bewilderment, relief, guilt. I sit and shiver under a cold sweat and hold on to Bianca as if she'll disappear if I loosen my grip even a little.

My sister's leaden feet make us both stumble every other step when I walk her to the bank of elevators in my building after the kind cabbie drops us off, leaving us to our devices with a hefty tip from me for his trouble. Bianca keeps mumbling something I can't make out but doesn't respond when I ask her what she's saying.

She's still out of it, but she can at least be useful. Still barefoot, I hook the straps of my heels through a couple of her fingers as I unlock my apartment door and usher her inside.

After I settle Bianca on the couch, I hit my feet with lots of soap, water and alcohol before I return to try and make my sister comfortable.

I freeze with wide eyes in the process of trying to get off her coat. What the hell... her outfit is skimpier than mine, jet black and more cutout than solid fabric. The hem barely reached her hips.

Perhaps she senses my confusion because her eyes open to slits and she looks up at me standing over her. Frowning, she wets her lips. "What the hell are you wearing?" she says, then goes limp as she tumbles back into sleep.

If she had been fully lucid when she asked, I still wouldn't have had a good answer for her.

Shaken, I curl up on the other end of the couch, hugging my knees to my chest.

CHAPTER

Twelve

After making sure my sister is truly down for the count, I take the quickest possible shower I can, running my soapy hands over my naked flesh without lingering over the task any longer than necessary. For now, I need to forget about the feel of hands all over my body that don't belong to me, stroking and rubbing solely to bring me pleasure.

Not for the first time, a shudder wracks my bones when I think of what could have happened to Bianca because I'd *insisted* on going to the BDSM club tonight. True, I could have been occupied by anything else, like a date or a movie or a grocery store run, but if I had, there's no way I would have been separated from my phone for hours the way I was at the club. Bianca would have been able to reach me otherwise, and that knowledge makes something shrivel up inside me from the shame.

Someone had dumped her at a bus stop, probably at the same time J and Nikki had their –

I run a clawed hand through clumps of my wet curls. What am I doing?

After slipping into a set of cotton pajamas, I pad barefoot and clean back out to the living room to try and get Bianca into the bed in my guestroom. It's dark in here, save for the tiny light above the stove and the small lamp on the end table near the end of the couch by Bianca's feet.

She's finally stopped groaning in her sleep. The deep furrow that marked her brow for the first hour or so I watched her on the couch is gone now, her face relaxed and almost dreamy. A wistful smile touches my lips. She sleeps curled into a ball, just like I do. I don't have the heart to wake her.

A resigned sigh escapes me as fatigue settles deep into my muscles. It's late – or rather, very early. There's no point in trying to sleep, though. My body may be tired, but my mind is firing on all cylinders, my thoughts ceaseless and irritating enough to keep me awake for hours yet.

I tiptoe to the armchair next to the couch, my eyes still glued to my sleeping sister. She still hasn't woken up long enough to tell me what had happened to her that made her reach out to me so urgently. Honestly, I don't know that she will tell me anyway at this point, especially considering the state I found her in, but I can hope she will once she wakes.

God, so many times when I was Bianca's age, I wished for an older sister to look up to, to model myself after. I could never count all the stupid decisions I made when I was her age just trying to figure out life as I went along, with my love life in particular. If I had had an older sister watching out for me, I imagine my life in that department would be very different. And I'd have far fewer emotional scars to deal with to this day.

All I've ever wanted was to be the kind of big sister I had wanted so badly as a kid. Tonight, I failed at that in a major way.

Plugged in to the charger on the end table between the couch and my chair, I glance at my cell and my stomach twists hard.

Both J and Nikki have called and sent texts asking if I'm okay. Everything feels too raw still to speak to either of them, so I don't respond, but I will tomorrow. Maybe.

Letting my head fall back against the soft back of my overstuffed chair, I study Bianca's face and try to imagine myself in her shoes tonight. That outfit belonged on a sex worker, not my little sister. She and I have both inherited our mother's curves, but cold weather or not, Bianca had her coat so buttoned up it's clear she was trying to hide all of that. She wasn't comfortable in it.

I hate to admit it, but I was starting to resent being the one who called all the time to check on her. I didn't like the way it made me feel – overbearing and lonely. But look what happens when I let up a little: our family's little girl, vulnerable and twisting in the wind in NYC.

A loud yawn startles me and I jump. Must have fallen asleep.

Once I finish rubbing my eyes, a quick glance at the wall clock in the kitchen confirms it has only been a couple of hours since I came into the living room.

When I turn back, I look up to find Bianca's sleepy gaze directed at me.

I'm on my feet and seated next to her in an instant. "Hey… how are you feeling?" I reach out to smooth her wild hair away from her face.

I'm unprepared for the sting when she averts her eyes and shifts away from me. She swallows visibly before she finally speaks. "How did I get here?"

I withdraw and clasp my hands in my lap. "I found you at a bus stop in the middle of the night, passed out drunk."

Her eyes flick back to mine at that. "*How* did you find me, exactly?"

"You shared your location," I say, gesturing at my phone on its charger.

"Oh." She drew her legs up, curling in on herself and staring into the center of the room, unseeing.

Bianca doesn't speak for a long while. I don't want to rush her since she's clearly on edge and fragile. But I need answers.

"Bianca," I begin, voice soft as I tread carefully, "nothing about earlier tonight makes any sense. You about scared me to death. What happened?"

She sighs and I can see her body shudder with the exhalation as she closes her eyes… as if the unspoken answer to my question causes her physical pain.

"Bianca, look at me."

With clear reluctance, my sister's eyes shift to look at mine.

"What happened? What made you send me that text?"

"Fine." Bianca pulls her knees even closer to her chest, making herself smaller.

I hold my breath.

"There was this… party. Upper East Side, with some people from my classes. A guy that I… like, was going to be there, which is why I wanted to go in the first place. Because he'd asked me to." Pausing, she rubs at the back of her neck.

At the risk of killing her story on the vine, I interrupt her. "Is this someone you've been talking to for a while?" I think of her obsession with her phone, like she was always waiting for contact with someone that never came when she needed it. The wait itself destroying her confidence in herself.

To my great relief, Bianca simply nodded. "Yeah, for a while. Anyway, he was there but he ignored me the whole time. The people I thought were friends did, too." She shrugs and my heart aches at the sheen of tears in her eyes she won't shed. "The guy I had been talking to ended up taking another girl upstairs at the party. I thought I was… in, I guess. And I wasn't. So, I drank a bunch out of the first liquor bottle I saw and wandered around until… I guess until you found me."

I gape at her, aghast. It takes a tremendous amount of effort to keep my voice even and calm. "Bianca, do you have any idea how dangerous that was?"

"I was too drunk to care." She winces and passes a hand over her forehead. "I think I still am, honestly."

"*I* care, B. Mommy cares. Derrick cares. We all love you too much for you to act this reckless." When I glance down, my hands are gripping the seat cushions so hard my knuckles start turning white.

My chest physically hurts, my heart aches for her so badly. I've been there, more times than I care to remember. I remember vividly how painful it is to be rejected and abandoned by someone you care about. "You know you could have talked to me about all this, right?" I hope she does with all my being.

That look in her eyes turns steely when she looks at me. "You always seemed pretty busy to me."

Ouch – shots fired. There it is, the resentment she carries for me.

I can't have that.

This time, I grab her hand and don't let go when she tries to pull away again. "Listen to me: I'm sorry. I get so caught up in my own life and issues sometimes…" I hang my head. "It's no excuse. I should have been there more for you as your sister. And as your friend. I'm sorry for that."

Bianca stays quiet for longer than I expect, but then she does something I don't expect at all – leaning over, she wraps her thin arms around my middle and hugs me, making my brows shoot for my hairline. When she squeezes me tighter, I hear the sob she tries to muffle against my shoulder and my own eyes fill up with hot tears.

"Oh, baby girl." I squeeze her back just as hard, trying to infuse my love right through her clothes so she doesn't feel so alone. She doesn't have to hurt quite so much if she has me.

We stay that way for a long time. I can't remember the last time we did this. Have we ever? I don't think we have, for sure not as adults. The sweetness of her being so close and trusting me with her intimate feelings makes me feel ten feet tall.

I hold her until she pulls back on her own and thumb her tears away on her cheeks. Holding her face in my hands, I look at her and say, "Fuck that guy," and she bursts out laughing.

It does my heart so good to see her smile again. I didn't realize it had been so long since I've seen it.

"How do you feel about a grilled cheese to soak up all that alcohol?"

Giggling into her sleeve as she wipes at her eyes, Bianca nods. "That sounds amazing."

"Good." I grin at her, feeling a hundred pounds lighter, and bounce into the kitchen.

Though it barely takes fifteen minutes to throw the sandwich together and plate it, I find my sister passed out on the couch again by the time I return. Poor thing. With everything she went through in the last day or so, she has to be wiped out.

The doorbell buzzes as soon as I set the plate on the coffee table before her and cover it with a tissue for her to snack on once she wakes up. I walk over and press the call button.

"Who is it?"

"It's me, Gorgeous. Can you let me up?"

My stomach flutters. With everything going on with Bianca, I had actually forgotten the happenings at the club for a little while. Reality is determined to make me face it before I lay down to sleep today.

I swallow hard and suck in a deep breath. "Yeah, J… come on up."

When I open the door for him a few minutes later, J pulls me against him in a hug that warms me down to my toes.

"Are you okay?" He speaks into my hair and squeezes me so tightly I can barely breathe. "Is your sister okay?"

"Yeah, we're both fine." I pull back to offer a smile up to him and he instantly returns it. My fingers drift over the gorgeous lines of his face as I stare up into dark brown eyes that have seen every part of me, even parts I didn't know existed. From the tightness around his eyes, it looks like he's really been worried about me – about us – tonight.

Then a shadow of uncertainty passes over his face, and I know J and I thought of Nikki at the exact same time.

I don't bring her up and neither does he. That's a challenge to tackle on another day; I've had enough excitement for one evening, thank you very much.

Instead, I give him a general overview of what Bianca told me, leaving out the bits I feel she wouldn't want to be told to a stranger. "She went to a party and got lost. I found her waiting at a bus stop."

J nods. It's a good enough explanation for him and I'm relieved. "I'm glad you found her when you did. It's dangerous in the streets at night for a young woman."

"For anybody, really." I nuzzle his chest as we stand there in the foyer, soaking up some comfort of my own.

The shuffle of feet behind me brings my head around. Bianca has roused herself and stands there munching on her sandwich, crumbs gathering on the tile floor around her bare toes. She arches an eyebrow and gives J an appraising look. "And who's this, dear sister?"

I snort at her antics, shaking my head. She's already getting back to normal.

"This is J," I say, looking up at him with a secret smile. I can't believe my man is standing in my home with my sister staring at him, but here we are. This is definitely not how I expected this night to go. "He's my boyfriend."

I cringe when I say the title, expecting J to tense against me, but he beams instead and squeezes me again.

Bianca yawns, then nods. "Alright then," she says, and wanders back to the couch, licking grease from her fingertips.

Turning back to J, I lace my fingers behind his back. "You want some breakfast?"

"Yeah," he says, winking at me, "I could eat a little something."

"Okay."

I'm sauntering away when I feel his hand on my arm.

"Wait – this was at your door when I came up." He hands me a small package, simply wrapped in brown paper. No address, no postage.

J heads to the kitchen while I stare at it in my hands.

Too small to be a bomb… probably fine to open it.

When I do, out tumble a pair of panties. "What in the world…" Lacy and pink, with a wet spot on the crotch I accidentally brush with my thumb. It's *sticky*.

Just when I'm about to chuck the whole thing across the room in horror, I see the note that had been tucked into the wrapper. My heart drops into my stomach like a stone when I recognize the handwriting:

Brooklyn,

Tonight was everything I dreamed it would be.

Can't wait to taste you again… without you know who.

Love,

Nikki

About the Author

Brooke Dean is a mother, story teller, content creator, producer, editorial operations manager - and now author - with over 20 years of television and digital media experience having worked at MSNBC, A+E Television Networks and Audible, Inc. where she produced the bestselling audiobook *Force of Beauty: A Newark Family Memoir* by Mikki Taylor. A native Philadelphian now a NYC transplant, Brooke currently resides in Queens with her son Jaxon, who is also the author of the children's book series *The Whisker Gang.*

www.brookeddean.com

www.ingramcontent.com/pod-product-compliance
Lightning Source LLC
Chambersburg PA
CBHW040910010826
48978CB00013BB/1224